THE CALL OF THE HELIX

A great sailor emerges
Is it belief, genes or imagination?

To Anne,
Keep on Sail &
Enjoy
Jack.

By

Jack Hermiston

Jack Hermiston
14 Mill Crescent,
Charleston,
North Kessock.
By Inverness
IV1 3XY

Cover design from an idea
By Donald McKenzie B.A. (Hons) M.A.

Dedicated to the Royal Findhorn Yacht Club
Where I learned my craft

and

to my four grand children, Tove, Jay, Fergus and Sam
who contributed more than they know towards the
compilation of this book.

and

with grateful acknowledgement of the advice
received from Elizabeth Sutherland and Murdo Grant and
the late May Marshall – experts all.

THE CALL OF THE HELIX

The Sennachie's Tale

I knew these young people and
the way they chose to go.
Their road was long and
hard and strewn with rocks
and shoals and pitfalls.
They faced their problems,
as they came, with care and
foresight, determination
and élan. They were not too
proud to seek the help they
needed and found succour in the past.
All were members of a team,
but out in front a genius was
emerging, perhaps a product
of his past, to reach to reach a level
beyond the imagination of the others.
My tales will tell it all if you
follow each step as it unfolds.

THE CALL OF THE HELIX

CONTENTS

THE CALL OF THE HELIX

PART ONE

THE BEGINNING

Imagination is but another name for power.

The Sennachie of the Ri
- The Sea Kings of the
Western Seas.

Chapter 1 The Skull Grinned

Scud stared in horror then yelled, 'No! Don't do that!'

He was standing at the edge of the sea-loch when two men pushed a boat into the water just where the bay poured into the sea.

'Come back!' he shouted. 'It's dangerous. You'll be carried out.'

But they ignored him and rowed into the middle of the loch. When the strong ebb tide caught them they were swept violently through the narrow gap and promptly capsized.

'Fergus, Ferrie!' shouted Scud, this time to his eldest brother who was working on their Dad's old boat.

'There's a capsize in the mouth.'

In moments, working as one, they pulled up sails, launched and were off. To the left of the narrows the rocks reached into the water and to the right mussel beds and sand barred their way with enough spray and turmoil to challenge any boat.

The tide pulled them out to the stricken craft, but clashing wind and waves created a maelstrom of frenzied water that taxed their skill to the limit. Shuddering to a stop and struggling for control they hauled the soaked and half drowned men aboard.

The task was now to reach the shore. They went about and prepared to sail against the tide. The two sodden bodies at their feet made movement clumsy, dangerous and fraught. The rocks loomed large in haze and spume and matched at the other side by the shallows which threatened to leave them stuck on sand. Water came on board in solid sheets and the boat seemed fragile and unstable.

But skill prevailed and eventually in calmer water at the slip they dumped the men on shore and told them they would be lucky if they ever saw their boat again.

'Why do people keep doing that?' said Scud. 'Goin' there on the ebb must be about the daftest thing you can do in a rowing boat.'

'They'll be reporters trying to find the lost villages or somebody looking for treasure in the sands,' said Fergus. 'It's an old village and when the originals were buried in the sand they moved it in here'

'They'll no' find much out there,' said Scud. 'They'd be better trying for the old ice house that's somewhere up river.'

'How do you know?'

'Just know,'

'Well anyway,' said Fergus, 'get the boat tied up. If we're helpin' Mairi and Pete collect driftwood, we'd better be off.'

Fergus and Scud were two brothers who with their sister, Mairi and brother Pete, had lived all their lives at the side of a sea-loch where the water rushed in and out with the tide. There was a big forest up one side and Chree, their village, was on the other. When the wind blew with a high tide they knew you had to look out for even the piers could be covered with water. When it blew from the west sometimes you could not see anything for spindrift and that could be dangerous. In summer the water was often like glass and the boats would glide across the surface until a little wind bent by the bordering trees, hurried them along. What you never did was go out on an ebb tide into the narrow opening to the sea.

Fergus or Ferrie, so called when fear or excitement overtook the others, was the oldest of the siblings. His skill with boats placed him in the van and muscled arms and legs were testament to all the sailing he had done. He didn't say a lot except about sailing or when keeping Scud in order, but when he did his word was law. But ginger haired, freckled faced Scud, the youngest, stood out and had a strange prescience and knowledge well beyond the understanding of the others. Possessed of a vivid imagination some called him a "dreamer", but his father used to say as long as he is a "doer" as well, imagination will get him everywhere.

But do not get it wrong, Scud was on the way to becoming a great sailor. He was lean and athletic with a dancer's build and balance and he rode his boat with ease. He was the one with a bit of magic about him. He could do things the others could not do.

They were all sailors, but Scud was Scud and no-one ever knew what he would do or say next. He told stories and someone always had to ask if they were true. He had stories about magic, about sailing and about treasure. He also said he knew a girl called Christiana who was born 700 years ago.

Fergus used to say, 'Where do you get all this? It can't be true.'

Scud's answer was usually, 'Of course it is. It's on the stone.'

There was an old stone statue just outside the village. It was more of a pillar and it was very old. It was covered in little pictures of boats with sails and oars, of men fighting on land and sea and a lot more that were difficult to understand.

'Christiana, she's my friend,' Scud would say. 'She's a princess; she's got a band of gold holding back her hair. It's in braids with little balls of hair at the ends. She's beautiful and she glows.'

'I know, I know,' Fergus would say for the umpteenth time, 'you told me, but what about the time you said you went sailing with her. You couldn't have if she was born 700 years ago.'

Scud tried often to convince all of them that it was true, but for a long time they just thought it was one of his stories.

Fergus was sure that the figures on the stone were just decoration, but Mairi thought differently. 'That's how people wrote things long ago. It's like a book written in stone. We should try and read the whole story,' she would say. 'It's telling us something.'

Mairi was fair and slender with long blond hair and was everything a sailing princess of old should be – a beauty with a sailor's tan, a thinker with a brain to match.

Pete was a sailor, but with other important things to do besides sail and he knew what went on around him in the bay. It was difficult to say if he resembled a small, active monk or a more studious explorer. You would not believe what he knew when he got started on history or birds.

Clearly he and Fergus were dark haired Celts from a race that had sailed the seas long before their time, but Scud was something else.

Fergus and Scud hurried down to the beach to help Mairi and Pete gather the white, bleached drift wood that had twisted into queer shapes and which they sold to summer visitors. With Fergus and Scud up ahead pulling it out of the sand and Mairi and Pete collecting it in their cart they worked up and down the shore near their house.

'Get a move on, Scud. Here, help me haul this bit out. Might sell well.'

'Fergus, this thing is staring at me. It's a skull and it's grinning,' said Scud.

'Get real, Scud,' said Fergus. 'It's wood. Grab this other bit and pull.'

'No' that,' said Scud, 'this! Look at my feet.'

'What are you on about now? I haven't got time for another of your stories. 'Grab this and when I say pull, pull.'

When they got it out, Fergus called to Mairi and Pete, 'Plenty?'

'Yes, that'll do,' said Mairi.

'Fergus,' said Scud. 'What about the skull?'

'A skull,' said Mairi. 'What skull?'

'Oh, no' again?' said Fergus.

'Where is it?' said Pete.

'It's aw blethers,' said Fergus.

'It's a skull,' said Scud. 'Over here.'

The four of them gathered round a decayed, crumbly skull with holes for eyes and long rows of teeth menacing like some prehistoric monster.

'It's a sheep's head, that's all,' said Fergus.

'Too long and narrow for a sheep and too big for a fox,' said Mairi, 'look at these teeth - they're huge.'

'It's a wolf,' said Scud.

'Rubbish,' said Fergus. 'There are no wolves in Scotland now.'

'What's in its mouth, jammed between its teeth?' asked Pete.

'It's a wolf,' said Scud, 'and that's a polished stone – a healing stone.'

'You're away again,' said Fergus.

'It is very smooth and see the decoration along the side of the jaws,' said Mairi.

'There was a man called Fillan,' said Pete, 'St. Fillan – and his name means little wolf. He had healing stones, but I thought they were down at Killin. His arm was at Bannockburn with Bruce and Angus Og McDonald as a relic that was supposed to bring them luck. They say it might have won the battle for them.'

'That's what I'm trying to tell you. Ask Fillan!' said Scud.

'You dreamt it, you mean,' said Fergus.

'But what does it mean and how did it get here?' said Pete. 'It must mean something.'

'I don't know,' said Fergus. 'I never know when he gets started, but we've got to get this wood home.'

All four hauled everything home and stored it in the garden.

They were all hungry and knew Mum would have their meal ready and she was at the back door looking for them.

'It's dinner time,' she said. 'Where have you all been? Ann and Iain Hargreaves are looking for you.'

'We've been gathering driftwood,' said Mairi, 'and Scud found a skull. It might have been from a wolf.'

'Well leave that outside for a start and wash before I tell you about the Hargreaves.'

Ann and Iain Hargreaves lived in the village too and were born there where their father was serving with the Royal Air Force. Their father had a boat and they sailed with him.

Ann was dark, slim and spare – a runner's build. Funny thing about Ann was that she had a small purple shaped star at the side of her mouth. At times, you could hardly see it, but it glowed when she got angry.

Iain looked a bit like Ann, but there the resemblance ended. He was very quiet, but when he spoke you realized that he knew what he was talking about.

'What were they on about then?' said Fergus when they were all at the table.

'Get on with your soup first,' said Mum.

'Ann and Iain have been offered a boat – an old racing dinghy. It's been in a shed for years and needs a lot of work. They are wondering if any of you want to help do it up and race it with them.'

'That's no bloody good,' said Fergus right away.

'FERGUS!' said Mum.

'Sorry, but we're a team, all four of us and if you add Ann and Iain that would be six in one boat. It's impossible. You usually race with two. When would the rest sail.'

'True and watch your language,' said Mum. 'But maybe you should go and see them. It might be a chance to race your own boat.'

When lunch finished Mairi collared Pete. 'What about this skull then. How did he find a thing like that?'

'Did he no' just stumble on it,' said Pete.

'Well, I don't know,' said Mairi. 'The things he comes up with and he seems to have spoken to St. Fillan. What does it all mean?'

'I can't see Fillan ever being in the bay and who knows what it means,' said Pete. 'The skull looks scary though and they do have stones like that at Killin. We better just keep it and see what happens.'

'Well I hope it's not a warning,' said Mairi, 'and I'd feel better if I knew where Scud gets this stuff - look out! Fergus and Scud are off. We better go and see about this boat.'

When they got there and Ann answered Fergus' knock, he said, 'You've got a racing boat then.'

'Yes, it's not much at the moment but it could be. What do you know about things?'

'No' much,' said Fergus. 'Only what Mum told us.'

'You better come in then. It's all four of you is it?'

'Yeah, it's all four of us or none of us.'

'Come to our hut in the garden,' said Ann. 'It's nice and private. It could be used as a team place.'

'Iain,' she shouted, 'come to the hut. The Stodarts are here.'

The six of them trooped out into a wooden hut at the back of the Hargreaves' garden. There was a door in the fence so that you could enter without going through the house. When they all found boxes or garden seats to sit on, Ann took charge.

'The Sutherlands have an old boat lying about doing nothing. We can have it if we do it up and use it. It's been lying there a long time and needs a lot of work done on it. But it's a real racing boat – a G.P.14. It's wooden, and there are sails and everything.'

'Anyway, Iain and I thought we could make it a team thing to do it up and race it. It'll be next spring before it's ready. There's wood needs to be replaced and new fittings and the old paint and varnish to come off.'

'And you think we can race it with six people?' said Fergus.

Ann shrugged her shoulders and said, 'there's a lot of work to be done although we hadn't thought of six people in the team. Still if we all take fair shares things should be fine. What do you think, Iain?'

'Oh, it's all right by me. This lot will never come in unless it's all of them.'

'Seems a good idea,' said Fergus, 'but we'll have to think about it. I've never seen a G.P.14. They don't race them here now.'

The Stodarts filed out and started to talk as soon as they got outside.

'Right then,' said Fergus, 'let's have it. I like it, but what do the rest of you want?'

Mairi and Pete said, 'We like it. Let's go.'

'Scud,' said Fergus, 'pay attention. You're in the team too. Stop thinking about skulls and talking to dead people. Do you want in?'

'Yes, Fergus, I'll do what you want to do.'

'Well, it'll cost. You can't race with any old thing. It'll mean our pocket money and our earnings. We'll have to do it in fair shares. Everybody puts in the same share of their money. Agreed? Then let's go and tell them.'

'Anyway,'said Scud, 'you'll get to see Ann a lot. You think she's cool.'

'Belt up, Scud, you're too young for that.'

Everything was settled and a new bigger team was formed. It needed a team name. The Stodart/Hargreave team would not do.

They all solemnly shook hands, even Scud. For the moment it seemed the right thing to do.

Chapter 2 'She's a Beaut.'

Next morning, they met at the hut.

There was a buzz in the air. At first, they were all talking and no one was in charge. It was the Hargreaves' hut but there were more Stodarts and Fergus was the oldest. No-one liked to say what to do until Scud piped up.

'Fergus,' he said 'when do we start on the boat?

'I'm no' in charge here, Scud'

'Who is in charge then?' said Mairi.

Suddenly everyone went quiet. No-one knew what to say until Mairi spoke up again. 'I'll tell you what. Fergus is the oldest and the best sailor. If you all agree, I think he should be the sailing leader. For other things we work out what we are going to do as a team – you know we'll vote on things. Fergus, Ann and myself could be the helms and Iain, Pete and Scud, crew. What do you think?'

There was a yell because it seemed a great idea.

'What do you think, Fergus?' asked Pete.

'Yeah, that'll do, but when we are on the water the helm is the only one in charge. Okay?'

'Is that agreed then?' asked Mairi.

'Right,' said everyone.

'What do we call you then?' piped up Scud who always wanted to know things like that.

'You've sailed with me often enough to know it's what I'll call you if you blow it, but a team name's a must. We need a name. It's important. It's competition time now and we need to be seen as a team. Somebody come up with a good name. Anyway, it's time we saw this boat – now.'

The boat was lying in the Sutherland's garage covered in boxes and old carpets, but you could see she was a real racing craft. Scud could not wait and started hauling stuff off her and throwing it on the floor.

'Easy, Scud,' said Mairi.

‘Scud!’ shouted Fergus. ‘Stop playing silly beggars. Stack everything against the wall so that we can see it.’

They started and could soon see all of the boat.

‘She’s a beaut,’ said Scud and the rest just gaped.

‘Imagine sailing this,’ said Fergus. ‘I bet she can go. See how she flattens out at the back. She’ll plane a treat.’

The boat was 14ft. long and had a sharp entry bow. She had sealed tanks at bow and stern to keep her afloat if they capsized and a seat right across the middle. The varnish and paint were badly chipped and there was a hole in the side, but they could get at it.

‘She’s even got a metal mast and boom,’ said Fergus. ‘They’re new, but we’ll need to replace the rigging.’

‘What does everyone think then,’ said Mairi.

‘She’s a beaut,’ said Scud again.

Ann just sat down and sighed. ‘I never thought it would be as good as this. It’s a real racer.’

Iain and Pete were roaming the garage and suddenly Pete shouted, ‘Look we’ve found the sails.’

‘Bring them over then,’ said Fergus ‘and we’ll see if we’ve got everything.’

He laid it all out on the floor – sails, rudder, poles, paddle and all kinds of bits.

‘All right, Fergus,’ said Mairi looking at him and on his nod pronounced the official verdict. ‘She’ll do and we’ll make her better: wait till we’ve got her belting round the bay.’

‘Now a name,’ she said. ‘The boat needs a name and it should be the same as the team name. Any ideas yet?’

‘What about the Rockets?’ said Ann.

‘That’s no good,’ said Scud. ‘Sounds like a motor boat. What about the Skullers? Might bring us luck.’

‘The Skullers,’ said Ann, ‘that’s rowing not sailing.’

‘Forget him, Ann,’ said Mairi. ‘He’s just trying to be funny. He found a skull on the beach and he thinks it’s important.’

‘What about the Ospreys?’ said Iain. ‘We’ve got one in the bay.’

'Well,' said Mairi, 'that's no' bad - anybody against that for a name? No, then that's it. We're the Osprey Racing Team.'

'We'll need somewhere to work,' said Ann.

'Yeah,' said Fergus quickly. 'Somewhere near the water? There's Johnny Wilson's old hut. He doesn't use it now and if we do it up for him he might lend it to us.'

'Fergus,' said Pete, 'He's an old grump, always complaining and he smells like dirty cheese. He's always shouting at somebody and look at the sight of him. He's mad.'

'I know. He's a menace, but his shed is right next to the old slip.'

'Well, if you can stand him I suppose I can.'

The hut looked right across at Meigle Horn, an old house on the other side of the bay. It had its own pier and was surrounded by trees. Because of the sweep of the small bay in front of it the house faced south. All kinds of plants – magnolia, clematis, flowering cherry, honeysuckle – were cultivated by Captain Dunkeld who lived there. All the team knew him because he let sailors tie up at his pier.

'Well,' said Mairi, 'if we are going to ask him, let's do it now.'

'I can't' said Fergus, 'I'm crewing in the 3 o'clock race. What about tomorrow morning?'

'Agreed?' Meet here, Ann. 10 o'clock?'

That next morning they gathered at the hut. It was the first time they had met as a sailing team and it was exciting.

'Race go all right?' said Ann. 'We went into town and I didn't see it.'

'No, it was off. Too windy – I'm sure it was gusting six - but Hugh Smith fancied going out in that little Mirror of his and asked me to crew.'

'You didn't go out in that little cockleshell of a thing.'

'They're good boats, Ann. Small right enough, and we only got about 200 metres. Water was crashing on the deck and the boat was bouncing all over the place. Hugh was catapulted right in head first. It went flat on its side but I had a good hold and just stepped on to the boom. When I got her up again and Hugh aboard I was only wet up to my knees.

Who was it who said that a good sailor didn't get wet above the knees?'

They went off to Johnny Wilson's house, full of it and excited. Scud was bounding all over the place and Ann wasn't much better.

'Hello Mr Wilson,' said Mairi as Johnny's shambling figure appeared at the door. 'You know the old Sutherland boat. We're going to do it up and race it. Could you lend us your shed to work in?'

'We'll paint it for you,' said Ann.

'The old Sutherland 14 footer? It's rotten. Ye'll mak' nothin' o' that. It'll no' float.'

'No, it's not,' said Fergus. 'It's old, but it's all right. We'll do it up.'

'Do it up!' said Johnny. 'Ye'll no' do that up. It's a wreck. Forget it. It's got rot in the hog.'

'Rot in the hog,' said Mairi. 'What's that?'

'Ye dinnae ken what the hog is. Ye ken nowt. The timber that rins the length of the hull, ye daft gouk. Once that goes you've had it. It's got damp rot and it's aw mushy.'

That's rubbish,' said Fergus. 'It's fine.'

I'll rubbish you,' said Johnny. 'Get oot o' here.

They were devastated. Their dream had disappeared. They had not looked underneath the boat and the Sutherlands had not mentioned it.

'Can't it be repaired?' said Ann.

'Course no, it's feenished. Throw it away.'

A forlorn bunch walked away: no boat, no grand idea left.

Chapter 3 Someone must know what is going on.

Next morning the sun was out. The air had that pleasant chill that sets you up and gives energy to muscles still slack with sleep.

'Scud, Fergus, Mairi, Pete,' shouted Mum. 'When are you getting up? It's a grand morning. You will have to get up early next week you know, when school starts.'

Scud just turned round, looked at his brother and said, 'Fergus, Christiana says the boat is all right.'

'Wish it was but you heard Johnny.'

'Well, Christiana's got something to do with the boat or us or something.She says McIntyre the Carpenter says it's not harmed.'

'Scud, it's too early for one of your stories. Has this something to do with that blooming skull?'

Mum's voice came up the staircase.

'Right then, no more lying about - breakfast is on the table. Rise and shine.'

Down the stairs trooped the four to slump at the table. No one looked at anyone else.

'Whatever's the matter?' said Mum. 'It was the same last night. Not a word out of anybody and here it is, a grand morning, and look at you. Dad's away to work, I've got half a morning's work done and you lot are moping around here.'

'Nothing good about the morning as far as I can see,' said Fergus . There's no wind and nothing will sail the day.'

'You'll not sail ever unless you get out and get on with that boat you've been talking about,' said Mum.

'There is no boat, Mum,' said Mairi. 'Johnny Wilson says it's a wreck. It's got water on the hog and it's finished. Can't be repaired or anything.'

'Oh, I see what's wrong,' said Mum. 'Johnny Wilson. Don't tell me you've been listening to that old goat. He'll tell you black's white if he can moan about it.'

'You mean you know the boat's all right, Mum?' said Mairi.

Mrs Stodart laughed. 'I haven't seen the boat for years and I wouldn't know water on the hog from water on the brain. What I do know is not to take Johnny Wilson's word for much. For goodness sake, away and get it checked. Try Willie Black or phone Captain Dunkeld. They'll know about hogs.'

Willie, was a villager, old and grey now, but a man who knew all there was to know about small boats and Captain Dunkeld, a life-time deep water sailor, was still as sharp as a clipper.

'Come on!' shouted Fergus and they all bolted off.

'Breakfast – finish your breakfast,' said a despairing Mum but nobody heard her.

'Where are we going, Fergus?' said Scud.

'To see Willie Black,' he shouted as they raced down the street.

'Fergus, Fergus, look. There's Captain Dunkeld,' called out Pete. 'At the post office. Ask him.'

'Hello all!' said Captain Dunkeld. 'Where are you off to in such a rush? Never seen the like since the bosun caught his pants in the anchor cable.'

It poured out as everyone tried to explain.

'Our boat's got water on the hog,' said Fergus

'No it hasn't,' said Scud. 'It's all blethers.'

Pete tried to get in but couldn't and nobody made any sense until Captain Dunkeld with a voice like a foghorn, shouted, 'Hold up, I can't understand a word. Fergus, slowly, what is it all about?'

'Well, the Sutherlands have given the Hargreaves and us their old G.P.14 provided we do it up. Johnny Wilson says it's rotten in the hog. Will you look at it?'

'No need. Saw it three months ago when the Sutherlands asked me to check it out. Johnny is an old idiot. Water got under the varnish on top of the hog and it turned black, that's all. The wood is sound as it ever was.'

The four just stood there and gaped until a quivering Scud shouted, 'it's all right, I told you, it's all right.'

A quizzical Fergus, gasped, looked at Scud with an odd look in his eye, then thanked the Captain gratefully. Mairi knew something was going on but she only said, 'we'll go round and tell

Ann and Iain. They were disappointed and they'll want to hear this.'

'Fine, glad to help. If there is anything else, let me know.'

They hurried round to the Hargreaves and explained it all. In the hut they all started chattering excitedly until Mairi brought things under control.

'Great, we're back in business and we've got to get started. Meet at the boat this afternoon – 2 o'clock - and we'll see what has to be done. Okay?'

That afternoon they settled down to solve their latest problem. 'Right then,' said Mairi. 'We can't ask for Johnny Wilson's hut now. What do we do?'

'I've been thinking,' said Fergus. 'You know the long shed at the bottom of our garden. It's pretty long because one end was our old garage. We don't use much of the space now because of our new garage. I think Dad might let us use half of it. A screen could separate us from the bit where he keeps his tools.'

'It's kind of far from the water,' said Ann.

'Yeah,' said Fergus, 'but I suppose when the boat's finished we'll probably keep it in the club dinghy park. We'll only move it at the start and end of the season.'

'I'm all for that,' said Pete. 'Stuff Johnny Wilson.'

'Right,' said Mairi. 'Does everyone agree? Okay? Then we meet 9 o'clock tomorrow morning at the Hargreaves' shed now called Shore Base and now our H.Q. - if that's all right, Ann?'

Ann nodded

'O.K., said Mairi. 'So Fergus checks with Dad and we start from there.'

When Mr Stodart agreed they shifted the boat and Mairi made sure everything could be found again when it was required. 'We can get started on the repairs now I suppose, but do we really know what to do, Fergus?' It is a racing boat after all. Do you think we should ask Willie and Captain Dunkeld to keep us right?'

'Yeah, good idea, Mairi. It'll have to be well done for racing. Ann and you should ask them to come round. Agreed everybody?'

Mairi and Ann did that and Team Osprey got ready to come into existence.

That night Scud just turned over in bed, smiled and went to sleep.

Chapter 4   Who beckons next?

The team went about their business but a world of water, effort, exhilaration and the unknown was soon to sweep them up.

For now Scud had to go for new school clothes.

Ann had promised to clear up her room before the holidays finished. It always looked like a tip but it was amazing how quickly she could find things. She never understood why it had to be tidy.

Iain and Pete were off to find the knot which often waded at the water's edge during its winter visit. Although they were keen sailors they liked to explore the world of birds: the oyster catchers, the red-breasted mergansers, the redshanks. The bay was full of feeding and diving birds calling with their shrill and piping cries.

Mairi and Fergus went off together. They felt responsible as the oldest and Scud had been getting on to Fergus about learning to race.

'He's a good sailor, Mairi, but racing is different,' said Fergus. 'There are a lot of rules and techniques to learn and you have to be able to do them on the water, fast. He's young and it's damned difficult.'

'I know that,' said Mairi 'but you're the only one who's raced. Are you going to teach us?'

Oh no – least not on my own. The club's the place for that.'

'Right,' said Mairi. 'We better find out what's laid on. But you're not the only one worried about Scud: all this about skulls and knowing things. It's creepy.'

Well, I think it is a lot of nonsense but sometimes I wonder.'

'I know. How does he get to know these things from the past. Who tells him?'

'He certainly seemed to know that the boat was all right,' said Fergus. 'A carpenter called McIntyre told him but the carpenter here is called Gordon and he's not a boat man.'

'Pete says McIntyre was a famous boat builder hundreds of years ago.'

‘Mairi, this is ridiculous. I’m going to throw away that skull for a start.’

‘Don’t do that, Fergus,’ screamed Mairi. ’DO NOT DO THAT! What if there is something in it. Leave it.’

‘Okay, okay. Calm down. Let’s see what the club can do. We’ll try and work out Scud later.’

‘At Willie Black’s their problem was solved. The Cadets were starting training for racing and they would get what they required with them.

‘Willie,’ said Mairi, ’could you and Captain Dunkeld come round and tell us what has to be done to the boat and is there is anything we can start on now?’

‘Sure. We’ll come round, but you can start by taking the old paint and varnish off her. Your father will show you what to use but be careful of the surface. Don’t dig out any gouges.’

Next morning they met at Shore Base. Mairi and Fergus gave everyone the latest news. Mind you, Mairi had told Ann, Ann had told Iain and Fergus had told Pete and Scud, but this was official.

‘I take it you all want to join,’ said Mairi, ‘and find out about racing. But, you heard what Willie said about starting on the boat. We must have that underway before they come to examine it.’

‘Fergus,’ she said, ’Have you got the stuff we need?’

‘Dad has a great pile of it amongst his maintenance gear and we’ll get what’s required. I’ll sort it out.’

‘Right, so let’s get going.’

They started to strip the boat and it was hard work. They all took a section but it still took four weeks. There were groans and moans but pride as well. When it was finished they could not believe that wood could be so smooth.

They went to the club to join the Cadets as soon as it was announced. People came from all over, but a lot came from their home village. It had always been a sailing village and the piers held pride of place. It was not big but it had been important hundreds of years ago. It looked over the sea loch to a big forest and to its right the Firth crashed on to a seemingly endless beach.

You could almost see the furled sails of the old sailing vessels and smell the tar and fish if you let your imagination loose.

The Cadets were organised by a cadet master called Mr Roxburgh and his three mates. They were divided into three divisions and the Ospreys were all put into the same one. Fergus was made the Leading Hand with Mairi as his deputy. Of course as they could all sail they knew a lot of what was being taught. But they were amazed, apart from maybe Fergus, how much they didn't know.

The second last activity was always to be a fitness session – a run round the village – and Ann was like quicksilver in that first one. She was always up front. Scud thought she should be a runner not a sailor.

Back at Shore Base to recover they went over the morning's work.

'When do we get in a boat?' said Scud. 'There's no sign of that.'

'It's only the simulator until the spring,' said Mairi 'and we'll have our own boat by then.'

'A simulator,' said Scud. 'What's a simulator?'

'It's a practice boat on land on a turntable,' said Fergus. 'It does everything except go forward.'

'You mean it doesn't move,' said Scud. 'A fat lot of use that is: Christiana doesn't train her sailors in a boat that doesn't move. They just get in and row.'

'Who the devil is Christiana anyway?' said Fergus. 'No, don't tell me. I've heard it all before. But if this Christiana can do it better tell her to come and show us. Anyway, there are a lot of beginners and it helps them.'

'Right then,' said Mairi, 'don't lose your cool you two. Things are going fine.'

'I hope the winter's not going to take too long,' said Ann.

'Well, here's what I think. We keep stripping the boat, but as soon as Willie and the Captain identify the repair work required we have a weekend off. Winter's nearly here and we should try for a sail before it comes.'

'A sail,' said Fergus. 'You mean to somewhere.'

'Yes, up river in a boat.'

'A boat!' shouted Ann. 'What boat, what for?'

'Well, and Fergus listen. There are people arriving here all the time looking for old things. Scud found that old skull and keeps going on about this Christiana and an ice-house. She says we'll find something important there.'

'Treasure maybe,' said Scud.

'You mean go looking for an old ice-house that people talk about but have never seen,' said Fergus. 'We'd have to borrow a boat but we'll no' get there in a club Mirror, that's for sure.'

'Well,' said Mairi, 'it's either there or it's not. I don't know who Christiana is but Scud seems to know.'

There wasn't a sound from anyone until Scud said, 'That's right!'

Fergus kept quiet but Ann jumped up and said, 'Great and we could ask Dad for his Wayfarer.'

Pete just said, 'Could be an ice house up river.'

'All of us could get into a Wayfarer if we go easy,' said Fergus.

'It looks as if that is more or less agreed,' said Mairi. 'Pete and Iain, you try and find out as much as you can about the ice-house and let us all know as soon as possible.'

'An' Fergus, 'you plan the sailing, right.'

Chapter 5 The River Expedition

Next day they all got up with a real buzz.

Scud kept saying, 'I'm going on an expedition.' He told his mother three times the night before and twice before breakfast.

Ann was still excited and had even got her jumper on back to front. But she calmed down long enough to ask her Dad if they could have his boat and he agreed.

Iain and Pete went to the local library to check on the old ice-house and found that it was supposed to be up river somewhere, but it could be one of those folk-tales that people tell. There was an old ice-house in the village which used to store salmon, but the other one was a bit of a mystery.

When Mairi heard, she thought a two day expedition would be possible if they did it before the weather got too cold. Sailors had slept in Wayfarers at sea but the Ospreys could take tents and sleep on the river bank.

Fergus decided they should wait until Iain and Pete came up with something definite before he thought about how to sail up the river.

In the afternoon it was down to Shore Base to plan the expedition.

'Right then,' said Mairi, 'who's starting off? Iain, you.'

'Okay,' said Iain, 'this is what we found out. You all know the old ice-house in the village but there is supposed to be one up river but hidden somewhere. If there is one it is likely to be on the left hand side going upstream, somewhere near an old quarry.'

'What was that one for?' said an excited Scud.

'I'm coming to that,' said Iain. 'You know that the village was a busy port for hundreds of years with warehouses full of things from other countries. They used to have ships, deep sea sailing ships, coming in with goods from all over Europe. They brought wine and brandy, tobacco and spices and even camel hair.'

'Camel hair!' shouted Scud. 'What did they want with camel hair?'

'We don't know,' said Pete. 'It could hardly have been to keep the local camels warm, but you had to pay tax on things like brandy and the sailors who smuggled it in didn't tell the customs men.'

'Smugglers!'

'Yes, Scud, smugglers,' said Iain.

'What they used to do was bury the brandy at night on the sand bar outside the bay before going to the pier. Later on in a rowing boat they would go back for it and bring it into the village. It was dangerous having it in the village and it could be difficult going out and in through the gap at night so they got the local fishermen to build an ice-house up river to store it until it was sold. The fishermen told everybody that it was needed for all the fish they caught.'

'Of course, that was all nonsense,' said Iain. 'The brandy was put into a secret compartment and covered with fish. Eventually the customs men found out and that was that.'

'Well, there's something else there now,' said Scud.

Bringing things back to order, Mairi started to question Iain and Pete.

'How do we find this place? It might be anywhere.'

'Well,' said Pete, 'they'd need stone to build it so it is probably near the old quarry and we found that on the survey map. And if they had to carry cases of brandy they wouldn't want to go far from the river bank. There might be a big mound like the one in the village. We'll find the quarry, then spread out and search. Probably the ground from the river to the quarry will be the best place to look.'

'Well done,' said Mairi. 'That gives us enough information. Agreed everybody? Right.'

'Fergus, go ahead and plan the sail. Ann and I will arrange the food stores and tents and everybody should be responsible for their own sailing clothes and life jacket. Remember old jeans and trainers. You won't be in sailing gear all the time.'

'What about me?' said Scud. 'I haven't got a job.'

‘I think you should be Fergus’s sailing assistant. Once we’ve arranged everything it will be the responsibility of the two of you to get us there. That okay, Fergus?’

‘Fine.’

They agreed to go in four weeks time. It was the beginning of school mid term and the cadets were on holiday as well.

The Ospreys were still worked up a bit about the expedition. Half the village knew and the other half should have known because of Ann and Scud. They told everybody.

Iain, Pete and Fergus checked the ordnance survey map again and the quarry was hardly three miles up the river. It was 400 metres in from a small bay in the bank and Fergus said he could find it by taking a bearing from it on his Dad’s chart to a monument on the hill opposite.

‘It might be difficult sailing that far up the river,’ said Mairi.

‘It depends,’ said Fergus. ‘If the wind is against us and we have to tack, it will be difficult. Zigzagging up a narrow river won’t be easy. At least the river isn’t straight and the wind can’t always be on our nose. Mind, there are gravel beds but six of us should be able to push the boat through. There are no waterfalls or rock barriers.’

Ann had organised the food: Potatoes, sausages and a tin with a mixture of flour and dried egg for pancakes.

‘What about sandwiches,’ said Scud.

‘Sandwiches!’ she said. ‘You can’t have sandwiches on an expedition. Whoever heard of an explorer with sandwiches and there’s no tea-bags either. We’ll drink water. And I’ll have rolls and frying oil to prepare the food. We’ll make a fire for the cooking. We’ll cook on one of the metal plates with handles that our Dad used to use. We can boil water in his deep one when we need it.’

‘What about other drinks?’ said Pete.

‘There are no other drinks. Just water,’ said Ann. ‘This is an expedition not a picnic.’

‘Well, it’s a bit tough, but does everyone agree?’ said Mairi.

Everyone agreed they had to do it right and Ann had been given the feeding job.

Fergus had been to see Mr Hargreaves and been shown over his boat. The controls were a little different but nothing out of the ordinary. He soon mastered them.

Very soon the great day dawned. The boat was ready, all the food was in the rear hatch and the tents were in the forward locker. Their papers – maps, drawings and notes that Pete and Iain had compiled were safe in an old case and stored with the tents. With six of them in the boat everything had to be stowed away very carefully. They did not want things about their feet when they were sailing. The boat was tied up alongside the pier and they were to meet at 9 o'clock on the Saturday morning.

When they reached the pier they were met with shouts and cheers. The village or at least what seemed like the whole village, had turned out to see them off. It was a great village for making an event of things. Ann stayed on shore until the last moment and did the final cast off.

Chapter 6 The Old Ice-House

Fergus set a course for the mouth of the big river.

They were all excited – keyed up to be setting out upon their voyage. The scene itself was beautiful, the sun just coming up on water that was calm with little ripples of wind catching the sails to glide the boat upon its way amid darting fish and gliding birds.

Suddenly, Ann piped up, 'I see it – the entrance, on the starboard quarter. About two o'clock.'

'There's some kind of barrier in the middle,' said Pete. 'Do you see it, Fergus?'

'Yeah, I'll port it. That'll let me ease off the wind.'

'Fergus! Look out. There's a big tree floating to port,' shouted Scud.

'Got it, thanks. Everybody now, a weather eye for danger.'

They progressed slowly but soon passed the barrier sign. Scud felt sure it would warn off smugglers and was a bit disappointed that it just said fishing was prohibited without a permit.

The river was deep and narrow, but the wind was still coming from the side and Fergus could steer straight up the middle of the river.

'The trees are beautiful,' said Mairi. 'That's a stand of birch. Aren't they white and I think that's ash and hazel over there. Look, just on the right hand side. It's like a painting.'

'Yes, maybe,' said Ann, 'but that's Giant Hogweed right up the starboard shore,' said Ann. 'They're vicious. Look at them. They're six feet tall and horrible and they sting like the blazes.'

'As long as they don't walk like Triffids, we'll be all right,' said Mairi. They don't swim do they?'

Scud's voice suddenly broke the spell. 'Gravel beds, Fergus! – off your starboard bow.'

'Got them, Scud,' said Fergus. 'When we reach the edge of clear water, I'll put her up on the gravel and you jump for it. Everybody, stay on board till I pass the word.'

Scud jumped and, as the boat keeled right over, they all scrambled as far as they could to the other side and the boat righted itself. It wasn't well done, but they were too crowded for efficient working.

When the bow was into the shingle, Fergus followed Scud. The two pulled the bow up and the other four joined them on a command from Fergus.

'Right then, three a side to push,' said Fergus. 'Take your timing from me. The water's running through the shingle. The boat will move easily enough. Wait till I unship the rudder. Now, pull-and-push, pull-and-push. That's it, get it goin' - about ten metres to deep water.'

'Shouldn't we be singing something to help us push together?' said Scud.

'Nah,' said Fergus, 'only your dead friends did that. Just take your timing from me. Pull-and-push, pull-and-push: she's moving fine, keep it going and we're there. Right rest, that's it. Get your breath back.'

'Great,' said Mairi. 'That was fine.'

The boat slid into deep water and they scrambled aboard. Fergus and Mairi trimmed the sails to the wind and they were off.

'What a team,' said Mairi.

'Look ahead everybody,' said Fergus. 'The river is going to bend to starboard in a broad sweep. Get ready.'

'O.K. turning to starboard now,' said Fergus. 'Gybe: Gybe. Oh!'

Everybody ducked as the boom crashed over but they were on their way again.. They went round the bends as easy as you like and were soon sailing straight up the river.

Suddenly, Mairi said, 'there's that monument, Fergus. We must be getting near.'

Fergus lined it up on his compass from boat to monument. 'Still a bit to go,' he said.

On they sailed until Fergus shouted, 'that's it' and steered over to the port hand bank. 'Scud, you take the nose again, but take the bow rope with you when you jump. Hold it until I come out after you.'

'Is it not a bit unlucky to land on the port side,' said Pete.

'Unlucky. Why unlucky?' said Fergus.

'Left means sinister, doesn't it?'

'This is not Scud's pals talking now. The old sailing boats always landed left side on. That's why it's always called the port side.

Everything was going well. The boat was tied to a tree and when the stern was secured the stores were unloaded. The sails were taken off, the boat pulled up on a sandy bank and a start made on setting up camp.

It was a beautiful spot, partly in a crescent shape carved out in the side of the forest and partly with a green sward that ran down to the river. It was made for them.

'You would have thought one of us would have known of this place,' said Mairi.

With the three tents set up in a circle, a stone fireplace was built and they all felt like real explorers.

'Food first, I think,' said Mairi, 'and then we'll work out our search plans.' Ann lit the fire and fried sausages for them all. They hadn't seemed interested in food when they landed but the sausages soon disappeared.

At last they were ready and Mairi called a meeting. 'Any ideas? Pete, Iain, you?'

'We have to find the old quarry first,' said Iain. 'It's east from here. After that it's anyone's guess where the ice-house lies. I suggest we spread out in a line so that we can see the people on either side. We'll walk slowly east until we find the quarry. We'll search in the same way around the quarry until we find the ice-house. If it's there we'll find it. If it's not, we won't.'

'Right. Agreed?' said Mairi. 'Let's not waste time.' They all formed up in line abreast, about ten metres apart and started to walk inland. Fergus and Mairi were on either end and the rest in between them.

At the beginning they walked through grass and messy weeds between trees but that didn't last. It got harder with thick bushes and spreading trees. Sometimes they had to go round obstacles and they had to shout to each other to make sure they were still in line.

Scud kept thinking he had found it whenever he came on a pile of stones especially if they were on a small hill. Ann was sure she had found it when she stumbled into a big pile of rocks.

'I've got it, I've got it!' she shouted and everyone came running towards her. At first sight Ian thought she might be right but he decided it couldn't be.

'I don't think this is a quarry. It's too small. It's just another pile of stones.'

They lined up again and worked forward. The weeds were thick and Ann shouted, 'Look out for Hogweed.'

'We're too far from the river for that.' said Iain.

Scud was having a hard time – some of the weeds and bushes were like trees to him.

'There it is!' cried Pete. 'Right in front.'

There was a kind of hill with a lot of scree in front of it. Lumps of stone with maybe one or two hewn sides were lying amongst it and two rusty rail lines ran through the middle. There were even two old wheels lying on their side and the remains of an old bogie.

'This is it,' said Mairi. 'We've found it. Time for a break and a check up. Is everyone all right? Scud, your legs looked scraped.'

'No, no, Mairi. I'm fine. It's only scratches. Could do with a drink though.'

Ann had brought some from the boat and then they were off again.

'The ice-house will be somewhere near,' said Mairi. 'Iain, Pete, what do we do now?'

'We've come from the west and it's not there,' said Iain. 'North and south next and use the same method?'

They didn't find anything remotely like an ice-house and returned each time to the quarry.

‘That leaves only the east to check,’ said Mairi. 'Maybe we should leave that till tomorrow morning.’

‘I want to carry on,’ said Ann and Iain who was in his element said, ‘let’s check the starting point for our eastern search anyway. I’ve got a funny feeling the place is near. They would use stone from the quarry to build it and they wouldn’t want to carry it far.’

Round they went to the east and in five minutes they found it.

They saw the stone arch first. It had been built over a gap in the rock to form the roof of the ice-house. They couldn’t see a door until Scud shouted, ‘I can see a little dwarf’s door at the bottom of that wall.’ He was all for clearing away the earth from the door that instant but Mairi called a halt.

‘It’s getting late and we’ve made fantastic progress. I think we should leave the opening until tomorrow.’

‘Aw, Mairi, can’t we just have a look inside?’ said Ann.

‘Well it’s up to everyone but there is a meal to prepare and I’m hungry. We should be fresh before we tackle it. You never know what’s inside.’

‘Mairi’s right,’ said Fergus.

Reluctantly everyone agreed and they all walked back to the camp excited by their discovery but dog-tired.’

‘I hope there’s not a dead smuggler guarding that door like in the Egyptian pyramids,’ said Pete.

‘A dead smuggler. There won’t be, will there, Fergus,’ said Scud.

‘That’ll be right up your street, Scud,’ said Fergus. ‘I expect you’ll know him.’

Back at camp Ann cooked a meal: baked potatoes prepared in the ashes of the fire and fried sausages again. Clean-up was a struggle but they managed it and fell into their sleeping bags.

In five minutes they were all fast asleep – just six bodies in a little camp by the side of a river. The moon was only half out and its shadows and the twinkling glints from the water placed a mysterious aura on their camp. They had stopped for the night but the water at their side continued to gurgle and toss and hurried past as if it was keen to get away.

Next morning it was pancakes for breakfast and off to the ice-house. They couldn't wait to clear away the earth and weeds and get inside. It took an effort but they got it open and Scud started in right away.

'Easy Scud,' said Mairi. 'Play it cool. Let the air clear a bit. That door will have been shut for a long time.'

'And say hello to that Egyptian when you do go in,' said Fergus.

When they moved in, Fergus and Mairi went first and shone their torches to find out what they were up against. They found themselves in a long tunnel. The north and south walls were natural stone with a mortared wall at the far end. It was maybe five to six metres long by three to four metres wide. The roof was hewn stone and was the other side of the arch they had seen from the outside.

'This is it,' said Mairi. 'Well done everybody.'

'We've got it!' said Ann.

She started to run round the walls and Scud jumped up and down with delight.

Before Mairi could say, easy Scud, there was a crash and Scud disappeared from sight.

Chapter 7 Scud Vanishes

There was no sign of Scud.

It was pitch black in the ice-house with the torch lights crossing and re-crossing in the eerie darkness. It was scary.

Mairi's voice, quiet and calm, suddenly cut into their thoughts as they struggled to work things out.

'There must be a hole in the floor. All of you stand still until we see where it is. Shine your torch at your feet and see if you can find it. But-do-not-move.'

'Here it is!' shouted Ann. 'It's at your back, Pete. Turn slowly and you'll see it.' He shouted out and they all shone their torches at his feet.

The hole was big and had bits of old crumbling wood sticking to the earth around it. When they shone their torches into it, they saw Scud lying on the ground two metres down.

'Are you all right, Scud,' whispered Fergus. 'God, I hope he's all right.' Can you hear me? Are you hurt? It's Fergus. You're in a hole.'

This time Scud replied. 'Yes, I think I'm O.K. Got a bang but I'm fine.'

It looked as if he was in a pit about two metres square. There did not seem to be anything in it except Scud.

'I think we should go down and check him before he starts doing things,' said Mairi. 'Have you got a rope, Fergus?'

'I've got a small one round my waist that'll do,' he said.

'Well, I'll go down,' said Ann. 'I'm lighter than you lot. Make me a bowline and slip it under my shoulders and lower me down.'

Ann was fit and athletic and she soon reached him. 'He's recovering and he's getting up. His torch is still working so we'll both search around and see what's down here.' She was soon reporting, 'we can't find anything. We need something to dig up the earth a bit.'

Fergus crawled out, got two sticks, sharpened them and passed them down. The sharp ends soon loosened the soil and they started grubbing it up.

'Anything yet?' called out Iain. 'I think it must be the smuggler's hidie-hole.'

Scud let out a cry and shouted, 'I've got a bottle with brown stuff in it. Looks old.'

'Careful, it might be smuggled brandy. See if you can pass it up,' said Iain.

Before they could do anything, Ann screamed, 'I've found a round thing! A button maybe. I think it's brass but it's a funny colour.'

'It'll be off a smuggler's jacket,' said Iain. 'Hand up the two of them if you can and keep searching.'

Ann and Scud worked their way round the bottom of the hole. There didn't seem to be anything else until Ann found a coin and Scud dug up a piece of metal. It was pointed but not sharp.

After a while Mairi called them, 'You've had a good search and we've done very well. Come on up and we'll see what you've got.'

Mairi got them all outside for some fresh air and a good look at Scud. He seemed fine. He was too pleased with himself to be ill. They were all excited but tired and lay sprawled around on the ground.

'Okay.' said Mairi, 'Where are we now? We've done well, We've found the ice-house and got four things that probably belonged to the smugglers. I don't want to leave but I think we should. And anyway I think maybe we shouldn't disturb things too much. The experts will probably want to look at it. Iain, Pete, what do you think about our finds?'

'Never mind that,' interrupted Fergus. 'Where's the treasure? Scud, your ghost woman said there was treasure. So much for her.'

'She never said treasure, she said something important.'

'Important! – a button, a bottle of old booze, a coin and a bit of metal. The coin might be worth something but I wouldn't give you much for the rest.'

'Still, three of them could be important,' said Iain. 'I think you would call them artefacts. They probably mean the smugglers used the ice-house but the museum will know.'

'Fergus,' said Mairi, 'what about getting back? It's two o'clock.'

'The wind is south westerly,' said Fergus 'and it will be with us. There won't be any tide if we go in the next hour.'

'Right then,' said Mairi. 'I think it's time to go when we've cleared up. Agreed?'

That didn't take long and before they knew it they were on their way home.

Ann and Scud were strangely quiet. The main finds were theirs and they could not get over it. Scud was disappointed not to have found whatever Christiana was talking about but they had found four things. Ann felt sure the coin was valuable.

Soon they were spotted in the bay and both sets of parents were at the pier to meet them.

'Are you all right?' said Mrs Stodart.

'Did you find it?' said Mr Hargreaves.

'Everything was perfect. We found it,' said Ann as she stepped out of the boat.

'You should see what I found,' said Scud breaking out of his, strange silent mood.

'Quiet, Scud,' said Fergus. 'Mairi'll make the official announcement.'

Mairi climbed on to the pier and said, 'We found the missing ice-house and brought back four artefacts. They might be connected with smugglers but we'll get the museum to examine them. Oh! And we found a mysterious hole in the ice-house floor. Scud fell through it but he's all right.'

'Are you sure?' said Mrs Stodart. 'Where are you hurt?'

'I'm fine, Mum. We're all fine.'

The expedition was over but there were still things to do. The boat was derigged and pulled back to the Hargreaves. They gathered their artefacts and stored them in Shore Base.

'That's it,' said Mairi. 'Well done everybody. Iain, Pete, will you contact the museum and get them to identify our artefacts. Do you know who to ask for?'

'Think so,' said Pete. 'We saw a Mr Turner before and we'll go and see him again.'

Mairi shook hands with everybody and said they should meet again as soon as they heard from the museum. Fergus was a good sailing leader but they all looked to Mairi when there was any organising to be done.

There was a bit about it in the local paper. They weren't sure how they found out but it was exciting to read. Then Iain and Pete said that Mr Turner wanted to see the artefacts and intended to have the ice-house examined.

'Now then, Ospreys,' said Mairi when they met. 'It's back to business. We have a boat to prepare for racing and Mr Turner wants to see the things we found.

Mr Turner came on Friday and the artefacts were laid out for him. He picked up the button, looked at both sides and put it down again. Then the coin but this time he exclaimed, 'Yes, it is a half crown from 1709. This is Queen Anne. It was minted in Edinburgh. You see that "E" beneath her portrait. That means Edinburgh.'

Suddenly he went back to the button and rubbed some of the dirt off. 'This is Celtic. See the decoration round the outside, and this Coat of Arms. I've seen that before.'

'The coin though is probably one of the last to be minted in Edinburgh. After the Union of Parliaments minting ceased in Edinburgh in 1709. I'm not sure what it is worth but we'll see.'

He kept going back to the button, lifting it up and laying it down. He did not say much except to mutter again, 'I've seen that before.'

'The bottle is probably brandy but we'll not know until it is analysed. It will probably be ruined as brandy. Still if it is brandy it is a link with the smugglers.'

'I've got it!' he said suddenly, as he picked up the button. 'It's McDonald – Angus Og. Wait a minute, could it be McRurie – Christiana of Garmoran. It is almost the same thing really.'

Scud shouted, 'See, Christiana has something to do with it. I told you.'

'A button,' said Fergus. 'Hardly important.'

No, it's Angus Og McDonald.'

'Are they valuable?' burst out Scud unable to contain himself.

'Oh yes, there is value here,' said Mr Turner.

Even Mairi was getting excited. 'Could you get the coin valued for us? You see, Mr Turner, we have a boat to repair and it will probably be expensive.'

'The coin,' spluttered Mr Turner. 'Not the coin. It's the seal. It is worth a fortune.'

Chapter 8 The Scourge of the Seas.

There was a silence in Shore Base.

They were speechless. A fortune; how could an old button be worth a fortune?

'Not the coin,' said Mairi collecting herself. 'The button?'

'It is not a button,' said Mr Turner. 'It is a seal.'

'A seal!' shouted Ann. 'I found it. It doesn't look much.'

Even Pete and Iain were staggered, but they knew who Angus Og was – a King of the Isles.'

Fergus, who preferred to keep out of anything except sailing, said, 'What has Angus Og got to do with smugglers?'

'Nothing that I know of,' said Mr Turner, 'except that he was a brilliant sailor. His enemies called him "The Scourge of the Seas". The smugglers might have found it first and then lost it again climbing in and out of that hole.'

'Did he have anything to do with somebody called Christiana?' said Scud wakening up at last and wishing he had found the seal.

'Christiana,' said Mr Turner. 'Yes, she was his cousin or maybe his second cousin. She was the Lady of Garmoran and a great sailor too. Her seal is quite similar to his one. But it looks as if it was Angus that was here. He certainly knew his way around. Look at the coat of arms on the seal. If you rub more of the grime off you will easily see a ship with furled sails.'

'So there is,' said Fergus.

'This was Angus' personal Coat of Arms and his personal seal and that is why it is very valuable. He would not like having lost it.'

'But Mr Turner,' said Mairi quickly, 'how did it get here?'

'We might never know. The connection would be the sea and Angus Og got around. But I'll get the experts to look at it and they might know something. Incidentally, it's not brass. It is gold. It will have to be sent to Edinburgh and registered as Treasure Trove.'

'Treasure Trove! It's real pirate's treasure this,' said Scud.

‘That might be how the skull got here,’ said Pete. ‘Angus Og had St Fillans’ arm. Maybe he had his skull as well.’

That was all done and the Ospreys got down to real sailing business. It was cadet work next morning and that was always hard. After dinner they met at the boat to strip paint but it was difficult to stop talking about the fortune they might get for the seal.

‘When do you think we’ll hear, Mairi?’ said Ann

‘We’ve just got to wait. It’ll take a long time and we don’t own it. If it is declared Treasure Trove, we’re likely to get a good reward though. It’ll be next spring probably before we hear and we’ve got other things to do. Willie and Captain Dunkeld could be examining the boat this afternoon and there is a lot of paint to come off yet. So let’s get on.’

Willie and Captain Dunkeld came an hour later and when everything was cleaned up the two men started on the boat. Mairi stood by to take notes.

After half-an-hour they straightened up and Captain Dunkeld said, ‘If you have your repair log ready we will go over things.’ ‘First of all, the external fittings have to come off and the wood examined underneath. You need new jammers and new bolts. The rigging has to be renewed. If you are going racing you better get a jib tensioner and renew all the rope.’

And so it went on. Mairi needed more paper and scary thoughts were entering her head – how much would all this cost.

‘Part of the gunnel is badly split and there is a hole in the side,’ said Willie, but we will show you how to repair them. They’ll have to be done properly to make the boat fit to race.’

The list grew longer and faces dropped and dropped. But they finished and Mairi gathered up her papers. ‘Thank you both. We’re very grateful. Will you come again when we’re ready to do the hard jobs?’

‘Of course we will,’ said Captain Dunkeld. ‘We look forward to helping you. Gives us old sailors something to do. Is there anything you want to ask before we go?’

‘Well,’ said Mairi, ‘there is one thing. How much do you think it will cost?’

‘Of course you will need paint and varnish too. Let’s see – about £300 should cover it.’

Everybody kept quiet until they left and then Ann yelled, £300! Where are we going to get £300?’

Chapter 9 We haven't got £300?

£300 was a lot of money.

The Osprey's were stunned but not knocked flat like the time Johnnie Wilson said that their boat was a write-off.

'Never mind,' said Mairi, 'we'll make it. Keep calm. It's not £300 all at once and we knew it would cost. There are six of us.'

'Well,' said Fergus, 'we've got our wood money and all the Stodarts will throw in their shares. That's nearly sixty quid. If we all put in half our pocket money we'll have a fair bit.'

'How much will that come to?' said Ann. 'Even with half our pocket money it won't come to £300.'

'There's the smuggler's treasure,' said Scud.

'Right enough,' said Fergus. 'I'd forgotten that.'

'It'll be a while before that comes and we can't be sure about it,' said Iain.

'Yeah, and the first race is soon,' said Pete.

Mairi wasn't pleased about how things were going so she stepped in.

'Look,' she said forcibly. 'We've got a racing boat and we have some money so let's get started.'

They counted everything they had and between them they had £85. It wasn't fair shares but nobody cared. Ann didn't like the Stodarts having to contribute so much so she and Iain got jobs delivering newspapers and threw that in.

They spent all their spare time that winter working on the boat. Willie Black, especially, was round a lot. He showed them how to do all the difficult jobs and it all went very smoothly until they ran out of money. Things got very fraught when it looked as if they would not make the first race.

There wasn't enough money coming in and they had nothing left for paint and varnish. Money from the Treasure Trove seemed as far off as ever and the boat used a lot of paint. They put on a coat of Mr Stodart's old paint but that was being rubbed down anyway. When they got new paint about six coats would have to be applied to make it smooth enough for racing. Luckily the two Dads were impressed by the way they had tackled the whole thing and lent them enough until they had money of their own.

But then the club issued its racing diary and suddenly the first race was only three weeks away. Fergus found out first and asked Mairi to call a meeting at Shore Base. This was crunch time.

'You all know what we are here for,' said Mairi. 'Racing starts in three weeks time and we have to be ready.'

'I thought the Cadets weren't racing until the beginning of May,' said Pete.

'I know and that is one of the things we have to decide. Are the Ospreys racing in the main club programme or just with the Cadets?' said Mairi.

Things went quiet until Fergus said, 'I think we should sail in the club programme as well as the Cadets. We can all sail. We have to learn to race.'

'The club races will be hard going, Fergus,' said Iain. 'We'll be up against all the crack sailors and most of us don't know that much yet.'

'That's how to learn,' said Fergus. 'We've got to race against them time and time again to improve. We'll get thumped but who cares. We'll beat them in the end.'

'We'll be on the shore most of the time anyway,' said Ann. 'We've only got one boat but I wish we had another one. I want to sail - not stand about.'

'I'm sure we'll get a club boat – a Mirror – as soon as we show we can race. Two boats will make a good start for the team,' said Fergus. 'But you are right. I vote we try and get a second boat of our own next winter.'

All that was decided, but there remained the problem of who would crew with whom.

'It's no' a problem,' said Fergus. 'We must have regular crew training together. It makes sense to have Mairi and Ann; Iain and Pete and Scud with me. Sometimes we'll change for lots of reasons but that could be our normal crew list. Of course Ann is entitled to be a helm and it could be Ann and Iain; and Mairi and

Pete. It's important that the two in a boat act together so it's up to yourselves.'

'No,' said Ann, 'I'd like to crew for Mairi and anyway Iain and Pete have always looked like a team.'

'All right,' said Mairi. 'Anybody disagree? That's it then.'

Scud went all quiet again but he was pleased that he and Fergus were paired up.

'Somebody told me about this kind of thing,' he said.

'Scud,' said Mairi carefully, 'Is this one of your stories?'

'Well, I don't really know who told me.'

'I thought not.'

'Anyway,' said Scud, 'this man fell out with his father who was a king and he was sent to live alone on a little island.'

'Scud, has this got anything to do with anything?' said Fergus.

'Well, he wanted off the island so he built a boat, but he couldn't sail it on his own. When a swan came along sailing beautifully he asked it to crew for him.'

'Oh! Scud, come off it,' said a weary Pete.

'No, I'm telling you. It glided and powered itself along like an old stately galleon in full sail. When it raised its wings it was something else. I would like to sail like that.'

'But the swan wouldn't help the Prince.'

'Crew for you!' it said. 'I'm better than you. You can crew for me. You can sit on my back and show me where you want to go. But I'm in charge.'

'Neither would give way and the Prince had to stay on the island. That's all I know.'

'Thank goodness,' said Fergus.

They were all at the Cadets that Saturday morning paying particular attention to the rules of starting a race. Fergus knew but it was all very serious for the rest and they all got a bit uptight. They let off steam a bit during the last exercise which was more of a game than a fitness session.

The Cadet Master put a stool in the middle of the floor and said it was a rock being pounded by waves. One by one they had to pretend they were shipwrecked and cling on to save themselves. You could almost see the water washing over them and the wind trying to tear them off.

It was a great success and eased all their tensions.

The first race was a week away and although the Osprey's boat was ready, it hadn't been used yet. It had been hard work and now was the moment. Fergus as the oldest Stodart and Ann as the oldest Hargreave sailed it to the other side of the bay and then Mairi and Scud took it out. It was Iain and Pete's turn but who was to helm was still not decided when Willie and Captain Dunkeld appeared rigged out in sailing suits and life jackets. Willie helmed with Iain and the Captain took Pete. Neither Willie nor Captain Dunkeld had been in such a small boat for years but they soon showed they knew what they were doing.

The boat had been well and truly launched and re-named the "Osprey".

They practised all week and prepared for the opening race. Mairi and Ann were to race it first. Fergus and Scud borrowed a club Mirror but Iain and Pete decided they were not ready to race and would stay on the shore to help with rigging and launching.

On the Saturday morning they all signed on for the race and tried to keep calm. Fergus was quite composed but even he was being very business like and purposeful. He had done it before but as a crew. It was a tense time – all the sailors looked like experts.

The morning was cloudy and grey; the wind was force three gusting four and that meant you had to know what you were doing. All the club sailors were out and they all knew Fergus – he had crewed for a lot of them. Scud took the good natured calls in his stride but most were directed at Fergus because Scud was so small.

'Is he your secret weapon then?' or 'Why are you carrying a spare rudder?'

With the course marked on the back of their hands, they launched their boats and made for the line but, of course, they had to wait for the starting gun.

When the first cannon boomed a nervous Scud yelled, 'We're off and we're miles from the line.'

'No, no, that's the ten minute warning gun. You've forgotten it all already. It's ten minutes for a warning, five minutes to get ready and then a final gun for the off.'

Suddenly there was a swoop. Four big boats flashed past going for the line as the final gun boomed. Fergus and Scud were near the start but pointing in the wrong direction trying not to be over the line. Mairi and Ann were miles off.

They were last away.

THE CALL OF THE HELIX

PART TWO

SO YOU THINK THE Ri IS DEAD?

Against the surge of the sea
The craft of heroes.
And the pull of the wind,
Strive and conquer.
Make your way to the heart of things
And find yourself.
My hand in yours at the helm,

Angus Og,
14th Cent
Sea Warrior
and King
of the Isles

Chapter 10 The First Race.

The boats were leaving in a stream.

The massive flow sprang from apparent idleness to purposeful attack. Some were badly covered from the wind by bigger boats; some were quite a way behind; but most had mettle in their thrust. There were those who were merely happy to be off and scared to move about too much and those who fought whoever tried to take their place.

The bay was alive with straining sails and water gushed at bow and stern. The picture showed a scene of racing at its best.

The Osprey four were at the back with Fergus and Scud in front of Mairi and Ann but with the bigger, faster Osprey slowly catching up.

'Fergus! We're getting nowhere,' yelled Scud. 'The Osprey's catching us.'

'Stop moaning. Concentrate on what you're doing. Just sail and watch that jib. Every inch counts and if you don't have a stiff neck at the end of this you're not doing your job. You've forgotten about our boat's big handicap.'

The girls were struggling. Ann was nearly frothing at the mouth and her star was glowing purple. Mairi was a bit scared. The boats milling about at the start had given her a fright and everything was very strange. It was not the kind of sailing she was accustomed to.

'Ann, we'll just try to sail the boat properly and see what happens. We'll try and catch that boat in front.'

Ann, for once, had to sit and do that. The boat in front was a Mirror and therefore far slower so they gradually got right up behind it.

'What side do I pass it on?' whispered Mairi. 'I've got to pass on one side or the other or I'll hit them.'

'Fergus said to always pass to windward if you can,' mouthed Ann.

'I know, I know,' said the normally composed Mairi, 'but the buoy's close and Mr. Roxburgh said to try and get inside other boats when we're trying to go round it.'

Mairi's mind took over almost without thinking and she swung the boat inside to leeward and shouted for room to get round. She was a lot faster than the Mirror and inside it so it had to keep clear to let her round. It was the instinctive sign of a real sailor.

'Brilliant,' said Ann, recovering her natural confidence in a flash. 'We've gained a place.'

'Yes, but I forgot the right thing to say was to ask for water when you want space like that.'

'So it is,' said Ann, 'but I'd shout more than that if they didn't get out of the way.'

They swung the boat on to the other tack and the boat went up on end. They were flung crashing but Ann performed miracles. She somehow hooked her feet into the toe strap and hung out over the side to level the boat and carry on.

The other two were sailing along quite nicely trying to sail efficiently and fast. Scud was watching his sail like a hawk and moving it fractionally in and out to keep it at full power.

'I see what you mean about a stiff neck,' said Scud.

'Keep quiet and concentrate,' said Fergus. 'Look! You've let your sail sag again. Concentrate – not talk. I'll tell you what's good and you'll know when it's bad. There goes your sail again, it's backing.'

The club champion was battling it out for the lead with the Cadet Master's two sons. Scud could not keep quiet.

'That's not fair. That's the Roxburgh boys at the front. They'll get a lot of extra help from their father.'

'Scud, if I have to tell you again you're beached. It's not a discussion group we're in here. Do what you're told or I'll sling you out in the middle of the race and carry on myself. Anyway, the Roxburgh boys are a bunch of idiots. They make mistakes like the rest of us, but they don't talk as much as you do.'

Slowly they caught up on the Mirror ahead. At the third mark it went too wide and, as it rounded, the wind blew it even further across. Fergus nipped in to take a place. Scud almost shouted out but caught himself. He just looked at Fergus and trimmed his sail for the next leg.

There were thirteen in the race and the Ospreys were eleventh and twelfth to the end. The club champion was first boat home but lost the race to the Roxburgh boys on handicap.

The two Osprey boats sailed to the slip, jumped out, held their boats at the bow and looked at each other.

They couldn't talk a lot now. It is hard to say if they were exhausted physically or mentally or just satiated with pleasure. Scud had never felt like this before. It was the exact opposite of the nervous feeling they had at the beginning. They were relaxed but exhilarated. They had such a feeling of contentment that it took them over and they could not say a word.

As usual it was Scud who spoke first: 'We finished a whole race, didn't we.'

'Yeah, we did,' said Fergus, 'and three boats retired so we at least beat five boats. And who knows, the handicap might move us up a bit more. The start was awful but we'll sort that out next time,'

'When is the next time?' said Scud.

'You can't wait, can you?' said Mairi.

Iain and Pete, who been up opposite the line, came running up shouting their congratulations. 'Well done everybody! You were fantastic. Liked the bit at the first buoy, Mairi and Ann looked like some athlete hanging out like that.'

They couldn't stay but Fergus got them to fetch the launchers and help pull the boats up the slip.

'What are we going to do with the Osprey, Fergus?' said Mairi.

'I think we'll have to haul her back to the hut, but I think you should arrange for a space in the club dinghy park.'

'It'll cost,' said Mairi.

‘I know but if everyone agrees I think it’s best. The chat is good and we’ll learn things. We’ve got to be part of the racing group.’

‘Right, if no one objects I’ll book a place as soon as I can.’

It had been a challenge. They had worked hard all winter and had made a start at breaking into the racing side of sailing. Although they did not say it out loud they were pleased with themselves. Scud nearly did but one look at Fergus stopped all that.

They were going to be good because they had what it takes to be good: talent and guts and graft.

Chapter 11 They feel great.

They all gathered at shore base on Sunday – the afternoon after the race.

It was another glorious day. The sun was shining; there was not a cloud in the sky and there was just enough nip in the air to make you feel fit.

The bay looked marvellous. The water shimmering like a mirror reflected the evergreen conifers and the russet brown deciduous trees on its bank. It was like a big photograph.

The Ospreys felt wonderful anyway and the scene seemed to blend in with their mood. They were on their way.

Scud wasn't saying anything, which was unusual. Ann was not jumping, hopping or waving her arms but she did have a strange expression on her face. It was like a cross between satisfaction and complacency – you might even call it smugness.

Mairi was quiet, dignified Mairi. A very intelligent girl, she knew how much they had achieved and how far they had to go. Fergus had worked it out in terms of sailing technique. Some manoeuvres had been well done – even Scud's jib handling - and others badly. He was ashamed of their start and did not really want to talk about it.

Iain and Pete felt part of it all. They had not sailed, but they did not feel out of it. They were part of a team.

In Shore Base Mairi took over. 'Well, we did it. Our own boat has been in a race again. What do you think?'

Nobody said anything at first and then the unnatural silence of the last twenty-four hours cracked wide open. The noise was overwhelming. Nobody listened to anybody. The roof nearly came off.

Suddenly, in a way that was unlike her, Mairi shouted, 'Shut-up!'

In the stunned silence that followed she quietly said, 'Easy, we'll never make it if we sail like that again. The start was awful and we were scared stiff.'

'Okay. The boat was ready to race and that was a great achievement but we were not. Fergus, what about the sailing?'

Fergus looked admiringly at Mairi. He knew a leader when he heard one. 'You've said it all,' he said, but he went into the good and bad bits of their performance. 'We'll practise and practise and practise and we'll no' be scared next time. We'll get in and fight.'

'Iain, Pete,' said Mairi, 'are you sure you want to wait a bit before you start?'

'At the moment, yes,' said Pete. 'We don't know who should helm yet. Do you think we could take the Osprey out one evening to work things out.'

'Sure,' said Fergus. 'Next Wednesday might be good. The tide's right.'

They all agreed.

Fergus and Scud were given the G.P. for next Saturday's race and Mairi and Ann would try for a club boat.

'Anything from Mr. Turner yet?' said Mairi.

'No,' said Iain, 'but our Dad spoke to an auctioneer he knows and he says things like the seal could sell for over £3000 - maybe more.'

'£3000!' shouted Scud and Ann together.

'It all depends on the provenance; meaning is it genuine.'

'And is it?' said Mairi.

'It's away to Edinburgh to find out,' said Pete.

'But Iain and I think we could find out the value of the coin ourselves. There's a book that lists all the old coins and tells you what they're worth. Will we try?'

'Oh, yes. We need the money for the boat.'

'Another thing,' said Mairi, 'It's the fitting out dance for the beginning of the season on Friday. It's free for cadets.'

'A dance,' said Scud. 'I can't dance. Do we have to go?'

'No. I'm just telling you.'

'Tell Fergus. He'll take Ann.'

'Scud! If I have to tell you once more.'

'Well, maybe we should wait for a cadet disco, but I've told you.'

'Now last thing. Fergus thinks we should ask Willie Black down to Shore Base to tell us about racing – you know little tips about the kind of things you have to do in racing. He's raced a lot and could help us.'

'Fergus?'

'Right. Willie would sort out some things for us. The kind you don't find in books.'

They all agreed.

Fergus asked him and Willie came down to Shore Base that next Thursday night. The days were drawing in and it was grey dark when they sat down. Ann had lit two paraffin lamps and it was amazing how atmospheric it was. Scud thought it was like being in the fo'c'sle of an old three decker, but he would have been pushed to explain why there was a lawnmower in one of Nelson's ships. Still it definitely looked like an old sailing store. They sat on boxes except Scud who had an old basket into which he folded himself and Willie who had been given a deckchair which seemed to fit him very well.

'Fergus says you want to have a blether about what happens in a race. We'll it's tough. It's like a battlefield at times. You've just got to fight it out. It is no good keeping out at the side or the back at the start. You might get away with it in some of the small races here but never in big ones. You've got to be in the thick of it to get a position on the line and that means fighting with other boats. The best position is usually the windward mark but everybody wants it. So be careful. Some sailors will try to make you hit the buoy.'

'What happens if they force you into the wind? That's no good. You'd stop,' said Ann.

'Don't let them. Stay where you are. You'll feel like getting out of the way when you're threatened. But don't.'

Ann started muttering that no one would make her move.

'It's not so easy, Ann. The other boat might be bigger than you. Just stay calm and don't let them scare you.'

The talk went on until Mrs Hargreaves brought cocoa and biscuits. 'Don't let them keep you up all night, Willie.'

'Oh, I'm fine, Mrs Hargreaves. I'm enjoying myself.'

'Still I bet a dram wouldn't go amiss. There is a man in the lounge with his tongue hanging out. Away and join him and this lot can get off to their beds.'

'Well, if you put it like that.'

'I'm off then, Ospreys. We'll do this again if you want.'

The Ospreys were full of derring-do and spirit.

'Nobody's going to push me out of the way,' said Ann. 'I don't care how big they are.'

Mairi realised they had a fight on their hands if they were going to win.

Fergus and Scud were both feeling the same way. They were not going to give in to weather or wind or other sailors.

When they were good everything would give way to them.

Chapter 12 He would rather die.

Saturday was very near – and Saturday was race day.

'Right,' said Fergus, 'we keep it simple. Just get up to the line at the five minute gun off to the side a bit and stay there. At ten seconds point the boat in the right direction and go.'

It worked - not brilliantly - but both Osprey boats left with the fleet.

'It's easy!' shouted Scud.

'No, it's no',' said Fergus. 'We were up but slow and no' in the right place. Next time we work out how the champions do it.'

They sailed round – did some clever things and some not so clever – and came in twelfth and thirteenth on handicap. Fergus and Scud beat Mairi and Ann but there was not a great deal in it. It was a very satisfactory race for both boats.

What was wrong was that they missed the Cadets and the division they were in lost points in the Cadet championship. However the buzz was that in a fortnight the cadets would have their own race. Some of the cadets were very young and could only crew and it was to be held over a small triangular course just to get them started. Iain and Pete were down to helm but Fergus, Mairi and Ann were asked to help get the youngest cadets on the water instead of racing. Scud was to helm a boat and, as he was one of the youngest, this was a real honour. The Cadet Master realised that Scud had done a lot of sailing. It was just that he had not raced.

'I hope I get all these rules right,' he said to Fergus.

'It won't matter in this race – it's for training only,' said Fergus. 'Just steer the boat round the buoys and trim the sails to suit,'

'I got told that I wasn't doing it very well.'

'What!' exploded Fergus. 'Who said that?'

'I got a sail on a ship with a single sail – a big square thing. The man in charge said he knew I was helming in a big race and he would help me.'

'But who was he?' said Fergus.

'I never found out and some how I never asked, but it was difficult. The boat wouldn't go through the wind and when I came round with the wind behind me we got flooded. The water came over the stern and guys had to bail out.'

'When was this?' said a puzzled Fergus. 'Is this one of your stories?'

'No, but it is difficult to work out.'

'You were dreaming.'

'I don't know,' said Scud. 'Didn't seem like a dream.'

'Forget it,' said Fergus. 'Just do what I'm telling you. Most of the cadets can't sail yet never mind race. Anyway you've got two sails and they are easier to trim than one big one. Just don't shout at your crew too much.'

At 11 o'clock the cadet race got underway. They even started it from the beach with everyone helping to shove the boats off. All they had to do was sail to the first buoy and go round a triangle.

But the excitement was terrific. It was a first real sail for most of them. Certainly on their own and with the splashing and the wind and the boats all crowded together it was an amazing scene. Two of the sailors even fell in as they were caught by a big wave crashing on the beach. But there were helpers standing by and when they were hauled out of the water they were roaring with laughter.

But most got away cleanly. One helper stayed in the boat for about ten metres, got it going and then dived off the back end and swam to the shore.

If the truth be told it was a stramash – a huge traffic jam – but once they got round the triangle and came in they never stopped talking about it. It was a wonderful experience for them being in a sailing boat and making it go somewhere. They felt in command.

After it was all over Mairi passed the word for a meeting in Shore Base - Sunday 3 o'clock. She was rapidly becoming in charge on the shore.

At the meeting she said, 'Things could go a little flat now unless we plan something for the future. We don't want to get stuck at this level. I think we must have something else to aim at this year.'

'Yeah, you're right,' said Fergus. 'We'll carry on racing and we'll get better but another big target is necessary.'

'Well for Iain and me,' said Pete, 'a good target would be to start racing with the club.'

'Yes, but we're doing that now,' said Scud.

'Scud,' said Fergus, 'every time you go off like that I'm going to shout "bighead".'

'Scud,' said Pete, 'I know you are racing with the club but we don't want to yet. We'll let you know and then look out.'

'Cool it,' said Mairi. 'We're a team. We wouldn't have got this far if everyone hadn't played the part they're best at. Still we need a new team aim and people can do what they want to do as part of it. Okay.'

'Ideas then,' she said. 'Anybody got any?'

'Right,' said Fergus. 'Try this. We enter for the Schools Championship.'

'What, for all the schools!' shouted Ann.

'No, for the the Northern Counties. It's sailed in Mirrors and we could get club boats. Maybe even borrow two good racing boats,' said Fergus.

'When is it sailed?' said Mairi.

'The last weekend in August, so that will give us time to get a whole lot better.'

'Anybody disagree with that,' said Mairi. 'Seems like a good idea. Wait a minute, Fergus. How do we get there? It's not being held here is it?'

'No it's not and we'll have to work something out. You have to enter through the school so they might take us. Or the club or the Dads might help. We'll see.'

'Last thing on my list,' said Mairi. 'Next Saturday is the Cadet Cup. It's open to any member under 18 whether they are in the Cadets or not. Are we entering?'

'Yes! Yes!' said Ann and Fergus nodded his agreement.

‘Well, I think Fergus should have Osprey. He and Scud are better than Ann and I so they should have the best boat.’

‘No Mairi,’ said Fergus, ‘that’s not on. Not for now anyway. We’ll take turns for the cups and it’s your turn for Osprey. We’ll borrow a Mirror this time and Pete and Iain can have Osprey on Wednesday night.’

‘You will take care won’t you,’ said Mairi. ‘There’s no safety boat then so make sure someone in the club knows you’re out.’

One thing was following another and they were getting very involved with racing and with the water.

They had lived by the side of the bay all their lives and knew its moods and beauty. They often felt the wind as it swept in from the south-west in great curves. They knew it too when it blew as softly as a touch of down and had to be sought before it could be seen.

They had watched the tide with all its power and marvelled that it never stopped. In and out it went, sometimes high and sometimes low, but always there. It moved at first as a stealthy, irrepressible force, one minute not in sight and then there it was creeping in tiny driblets round your feet, fore runners of its future strength.

They had often admired the border nature set around it all although they did not always see the picture as a whole. They knew the trees were there and saw the changes nature wrought but to them the trees were simply trees.

Now they joined the birds to swoop and wheel and with the fish they turned and glided round the bay. They became a part of this well-kent world.

Scud was too young to see it just like this but he sensed the changes that were coming in his life.

‘This is becoming quite big, Fergus, isn’t it. Saturday will be our first cup race and then a championship. Never been in a championship before. - have you?’

‘No, I haven’t, Scud.’

‘Do you think we’ll do well?’

'I think so. We'll try. Anyway, we're not bad and we're getting better.'

Scud liked to talk to his big brother like this, but he was not sure of things. He did not really know what was happening and his brother was important to him.

Saturday would be another big day. He could not let Fergus down – he would rather die.

Chapter 13 It feels like the End

Scud had gone very quiet.

'Are you feeling all right?' said Mum. She was not sure if he was sickening for something and he had been like this once or twice recently. Still she thought, maybe he's just growing up.

'No Mum, I'm fine. I felt sick yesterday but I'm all right now. You see we're going in for the Cadet Cup tomorrow and the School's Championship later on.'

'The Schools' Championship! You mean the competition for all the schools.'

'Yes. I'll be crewing for Fergus and I had to think about it.'

'First I've heard about it. You're too young to be going in for things like that. It's not good for you. You stick to the bay until you are older.'

'Aw, Mum. I'm Fergus' crew.'

'Dad, listen to this. They are going away to a championship and him feeling sick over it. It is not right. Tell him he can't go until he's older.'

'Mum, I'm over it. I thought about what I had to do and I'm just going to do it. It went away.'

'I do not care. You are too young.'

'Mum,' said Dad, 'let the boy go. He can handle it. There is nothing wrong with being a bit nervous as long as it doesn't last. Anyway, we'll go and lend a bit of support. It'll be fine.'

Mrs Stodart was taken aback a bit but secretly pleased. If Dad was for it she would not have to worry.

'Very well. If Dad thinks so. But remember; tell Fergus we want to know all about it. It's not settled yet.'

Scud went off to school, but kept quiet about the championship. He was learning fast.

'You in for the Cup on Saturday?' asked one of his mates. 'You'll get murdered.'

'No we won't. Fergus says we won't.'

'Don't be daft. It's under eighteen. There's four in for it who have left school. You'll get slaughtered.'

'Anyway, it doesn't matter if we do. I bet were not last.'

'You won't win. One of them is taking "speed".'

Next day, they were all up early. Scud had a big breakfast and the race was at 12 noon.

'Are we going to take anything to eat during the race, Fergus?' he asked.

'No we're not. It's a race not a picnic.'

'One of the crews is taking something called "speed" said Scud. 'Sounds good.'

'Good luck to them,'

'Will it make them faster than us?'

'Don't know. Doubt it. They wilt when the action gets rough. Makes them careless. And they don't train enough. Never mind all that. Be at the boat at ten o'clock. I want to go over the rigging.'

'Are we going to do something to it?'

'Check it for a start and I've got two stainless steel shackles to go on. A bronze one on a cadet boat sheared last week. Wasn't pretty.'

'I'm going to see if the girls need a hand with Osprey. You go and get the covers off the Mirror. And take the sails. They're in the back porch.'

Mairi and Ann were doing fine but nervous. They had rigged the sails the night before and left them lying flat in the boat. Fergus was not needed.

'It's windy, Fergus,' said Mairi Are you going to start like the last time?'

'Yes and no. I'm going to be up front but I'll try and time my run in. There's no club champions in this race so I'm trying for a really fast start right on the line.'

All the boats were out early waiting for the ten minute gun.

At the five minute gun Fergus took the Mirror to the windward side of the line. The wind was getting stronger and white horses were showing.

Mairi and Ann were in trouble. They were too light and could not keep the boat level. They had a big jib up and it exerted a lot of force.

Fergus practised runs into the line, but Mairi was content to be near it, hove to and waiting for the gun.

Fergus started to count down the seconds as he bore down on the line – 20 – 15 - he intoned and at ten seconds with a shout to Scud the sails were pulled in to bear and they made a perfect start.

Mairi wasn't so lucky. Just as she swung the tiller to come on to the wind a gust hit them and blew the jib sheet out of Ann's hands. They stopped dead and by the time they got going they were second last.

Ann was furious but they got stuck in. It was a battle. They were too light and the boat was continually on its side. It looked good and it actually felt good. They were battling it out but beam end sailing is slow sailing and not for races. They solved the problem but it still slowed them up a bit.

Fergus and Scud were doing well until they came round to sail with the wind behind them. Instantly everybody put up a spinnaker: the big sail that balloons out front and pulls like two horses. The Ospreys did not have one and were left.

Both Osprey boats were suffering. Fergus shouted, 'Get that jib to the other side and get the whisker pole in. All we can do is goose wing.' That helped but they were glad there were only two spinnaker runs in the race.

The two boats didn't do badly. In fact, Fergus and Scud were fourth and Mairi eighth. Out of twenty boats that wasn't bad.

The Cadet Master was at the slip as they came in. 'Well done, Mairi. Liked the way you trimmed your sail to keep the boat level. Got to do that when you are light. And Fergus, that makes you the fourth best under 18. Can't be bad.'

Between the after race euphoria and Mr Roxburgh's remarks they felt wonderful. They enjoyed the sensation of well being you get after battling in a wind.

But Scud was right on the button. 'We need a spinnaker. Can't race without a spinnaker. Have the club got any for a Mirror? And we'll need one for the Osprey.'

'Dad's got one for his old boat,' said Fergus 'but it won't fit Osprey or a Mirror. We'll discus it at Shore Base.'

On the way home Scud met his school mate. 'Told you you'd get murdered,' he said.

'Who got murdered,' said Scud. 'We're now the fourth best under 18. What about that?'

'I know, I know. I suppose it wasn't bad.'

'Wasn't bad! Fergus was brilliant and I was his crew. The Cadet Master told him, so there.'

Scud was just bursting with pride but learning to control his feelings and not brag so much but sometimes he could not help it. If the truth be told, however, he was worried that he would not be Fergus's crew now that he was so good.

They were all looking forward to the Shore Base meeting to talk about the races. It was true that Iain and Pete were getting left behind but it was their decision. They had watched the race and then left immediately on a bird watching trip. They wanted to see some of the summer visitors and were on the look out for pipits and sedge warblers.

All the Ospreys sat down on Sunday in Shore Base and started to talk about the race. They didn't know whether to be pleased or not. They had done well but they had not won.

However Pete spoke up. 'It was a fantastic result. It was the under 18s for goodness sake. And you're not that old.'

'Yes,' said Mairi. 'As far as the Ospreys are concerned it was something else. We've got two problems though. We need spinnakers and there is a weight problem with our own boat. What do you think, Fergus?'

'You're right, Mairi. I saw you struggle to keep flat. Maybe there is only one solution – in heavy weather we put in our heaviest crew.'

Scud felt terrible. He was the lightest. He wanted to be Fergus's crew more than anything, but Fergus wouldn't want to be in the Mirror all the time.

It felt like the end for him and Fergus.

Chapter 14 The Seal, Coin. Blade and Bottle.

Shore base went very quiet.

It had all worked out up to now, but you only had to look at Scud's face to realise that it could all be very different from now on.

Scud grimaced, 'Does that mean I'll no' be Fergus's crew anymore.'

'No Scud, it doesn't,' said Mairi.

'It must mean something like that,' said Ann.

'Why do we have to change anyway,' said Iain. 'Pete and I like crewing together. We don't want to change even if there is a hurricane blowing.'

Mairi was not stupid. She knew this had to be handled carefully.

'Fergus,' she said, 'how do we go about this?'

'Our teams stay the same – Scud and me, Ann and Mairi and Iain and Pete.'

'Well, what are we going on about?' said Ann.

'In windy weather we might need heavier crew in Osprey,' said Fergus. 'Horses for courses Dad calls it. There's no need to get all uptight about it.'

'But it changes all the time,' said Ann. 'We can't keep shifting about.'

'Okay. It's all to do with how often we change but we have to accept that there is a difference between the Osprey and a Mirror and a Force 2 and a Force 5 when we are racing.'

'Maybe for championships,' said Pete, 'but everyone has got to learn to handle heavy weather.'

'Right,' said Mairi, 'but there is another thing. Everybody has to learn to helm. Fergus. These decisions are yours.'

'I know and I'll deal with it. I don't want a lot of changes. I like crewing with Scud.'

Scud shrank back into the corner. Tears came into his eyes when he heard Fergus say that and he didn't want any one to see.

‘Week day races are starting soon and we could change the helms then,’ said Mairi. ‘But now, spinnakers. We need one for Osprey but what about money?’

‘How much will one cost?’ said Scud.

‘Don’t know,’ said Fergus. ‘Maybe £70.’

‘Phew, that’s a lot.’

‘I don’t think we’ll save another £70 this season,’ said Mairi.

Iain suddenly interrupted. ‘Pete and I might know how to buy one. Mr Turner says the coin from the ice house is probably worth between £100 and £200 depending on how worn it is. So that would buy a spinnaker.’

‘Fantastic,’ said Ann.

‘When will we get the money, Iain,’ said Mairi.

‘It’s at Treasure Trove now and Mr Turner expects a single coin will be returned to the finders to sell or do what they want with it. Not definite yet though.’

‘Well that probably solves that.’

‘The seal is different. There’s the provenance thing. Christiana of Garmoran is mentioned but it probably belonged to Angus Og MacDonald.’

‘Will it matter?’ said Ann.

‘Angus Og was more important. He was the Head King of all the Isles.’

‘Who was she anyway?’ said Ann.

‘Mr Turner says she had her own little kingdom, but apart from being Angus Og’s cousin I don’t know.’

‘She was a sailor,’ said Scud.

‘What!’ said Pete.

‘She was a sailor, a great sailor. Could beat the men. And she sailed Bruce to safety once.’

‘How do you know?’ said Mairi.’

‘I just know,’ said Scud.

‘We’ll ask,’ said Pete . ‘And if it belongs to Angus Og the museum might buy it and then maybe someone will fancy sailing us to the places where he lived.’

‘Another expedition!’ said Scud.

‘It’s a long way but it might happen,’ said Iain.

‘Is there anything about the other things?’ said Mairi.

‘They think the piece of metal is an old dagger blade and it’s being tested. They are trying to find out where it was made. The bottle is somewhere else but we don’t know where.’

‘Right then,’ said Fergus. ‘I’ve got something . The cadet divisions are sailing each other next Saturday.’

‘Is it a cadet racing championship?’ said Pete

‘It’s both,’ said Fergus. ‘The cadet divisions are sailing each other.’

‘Yeah, but is it an individual championship?’ said Pete.

‘Yes, but by age group. It’s under twelve, twelve to fourteen and over fourteen. I reckon it’ll have to be Scud and one of his pals: Pete and Iain and Mairi and Ann.’

I’m not over twelve,’ said Ann.

‘No, but Mairi is.’

‘You’re not going to race then,’ said Scud.

‘No, I don’t think so. We can’t crew together in this one so I’ll help out on the shore.’

The notice went up in the club with the entrants. Scud was with his pal Jimmie Scott in the junior race, Pete and Iain were together in the intermediate and Mairi and Ann were in the senior.

‘Who is A. Stodart? We don’t have an A. Stodart,’ said Ann.

There was an awkward silence.

It was Scud but he hated his real name. He was never called Adam.

‘It’s only his Sunday name,’ said Fergus, ‘but he’ll only answer to Scud. That right, Scud.’

‘But what does the A. stand for?’ said Ann. ‘Is it Anthony? I know, it’s for Cleopatra’s boy friend.’

‘If you must know,’ said Scud, ‘it’s Adam. If you call me that, I’ll . . . ‘.

‘ADAM! ADAM! You, called Adam.’

A body – Scud – just flew at Ann. He pummelled her shouting, ‘No! - It’s no’ – it’s no’. My name’s Scud.’

He had lost the head completely. For some reason he could not stand his real name. Even Mum accepted that and called him Scud.

'Don't call me anything else. My name is Scud!' he shouted.

Ann realized that this was serious. She had never seen him like this before and they really got on very well.

'I'm sorry, Scud. You're certainly only Scud to me. Mairi will tell the Cadet Master it should read S.Stodart.'

Things calmed down and the races started. Scud won his race and Mr Roxburgh said he was a champion in the making. Pete and Iain easily won their race but Mairi and Ann had a fight on their hands.

Duncan McKnight, their main opponent, was a good sailor. He made sure he was near the line at the start and although Mairi beat him over it he doggedly followed her every inch of the way. He even attacked on the reach with a terrific windward surge.

Taking the wind about a hundred metres from the buoy he moved ahead and forced Mairi to cling on. She knew they had to get inside at the buoy and fell in behind Duncan's transom. At the right moment she went tighter, swung back, took the wind on her quarter and dived inside her opponent's transom line. She had her right of way and Duncan had to let her round first. She stayed there until the end.

It was well done and The Cadet Master said so.

Mairi was improving fast.

Chapter 15 Scud goes Missing

Scud woke up with a start.

It was going to be a busy week. Mairi, Ann and Fergus had exams and couldn't race on Wednesday. Iain and Pete had to meet Mr Turner after school and couldn't guarantee being back in time to sail Osprey. And on Saturday it was the final competition for the Cadet Divisional Championship – knot tying.

Fergus had said Scud was good enough to helm if he could get Jimmie to crew but heaven help them at the knot tying. Jimmie was more than keen and secretly would like to be an Osprey. They arranged to meet at the dinghy park at half past six on the Wednesday of the race - no later.

Scud was full of it, but unknown to him Mairi had arranged a special session on knots with Fergus on the Friday night at Shore Base. Their division was the favourite to win the championship but they could be beaten. Scud was the snag. He was hopeless with knots.

When Fergus told him about the session he just groaned and said 'I hate them but I'll try like anything. Have you got time though to help me on Wednesday with the fairlead settings on Osprey? I'm never sure about that big genny.'

'You know the rule,' said Fergus. 'It's just the same as ever. A genny is just a big jib so it's right back for heavy weather and right forward for light and in between until the curve is right.'

'Fergus, another favour. If the Race Officer says it's sailable on Wednesday let us go. Never mind if it's a bit windy.'

'I don't know, Scud. Got to be careful.'

'But, we've got to learn to race in heavy stuff. I know what to do. I'll luff up and I'll work the main and you can put up the small jib if you want.'

'You're asking an awful lot.'

'You can trust me.'

'I could kill you, but I'll tell you what. If it's windy, I'll ask Dad. If he agrees, that'll be fine. All right?'

'Okay, but I've got to helm in wind sometime.'

Wednesday arrived and it was windy. It was bad during the day but it was easing in the evening when Fergus arrived with Mr. Stodart.

'It is windy but it's dropping,' he said. 'You might manage. We'll see. I'm off to look at the forecast and have a word with the Race Officer.'

In the event the wind dropped a bit more and Mr. Stodart agreed the crewing.

The boat was heavy for them and they had difficulty getting in. It kept slewing up into the wind. Eventually Scud got Jimmie in and simply dived over the gunnel to leave the shore lying across the boat. But he did have the main sail sheet in his hand and along with Jimmie on the genny they picked up control and speed. Once he set the rudder in the right position they looked a very efficient racing team. The boat behaved impeccably and raced up the bay.

The wind kept easing but now and again gusting up to force four. You could see it was keeping them on their toes. They had the genny in the jammers for racing speed, but Scud had to be like lightening on the main. It was out to level and in again in a flash.

If you didn't know Scud you might say he threw caution to the wind. He had sailed all his life. It was only this racing business that was different. He knew that one mistake and they were in but that mistake never came. They were doing well but, of course, some of the racing regulars were absent for a mid-week race. Anyway they took three places and were in third position at the mark.

The wind dropped again and their lack of weight enabled them to close with the leaders. When they rounded the second last mark the wind was quite benign, but as soon as they were clear and in to the run again it blew out of the south-west like steam out a kettle.

They did not have a spinnaker – thank goodness – but the boat in front did and it went over with a clatter. The Osprey's bow went down with the sails they had up and Scud screamed, 'back! back!' as the two of them slid down to perch precariously on the transom. Up came the bow and the boat took off on a plane balanced on its own bow wave. The Osprey looked like a speed boat with two enormous jets of water coming up the side. All the laws of physics seemed to be denied. The speed was phenomenal, but the risk was right off the scale. Scud kept the boat straight and that is what mattered. It was no mean feat. Mr Roxburgh reckoned only a champion of the future could have done it.

How they were going to get round the mark no one knew. I do not think they had time to worry about it - but the spectators did. And then fate played her first card. The wind collapsed twenty yards from the last mark and they glided round. After that nightmare round it was unbelievable.

There they were, on the last leg, lying second. They were not going to win but you could see they meant to stay second. They went to windward of the third boat and stayed there to make sure it didn't pass them. They were a study in concentration. When Jimmie turned round to talk to Scud you could not hear what Scud said but everyone knew what he shouted. Jimmie jerked his head back and kept his eyes glued to the luff.

But the second card was yet to be played.

The wind struck with force about thirty yards from the finish. They could not hold it and the boat went up on end. They sailed through the line – second – with the lee gunnel under water and the two of them perched on the other side.

To the sound of cheers they waved as fate played out its final act amid the gathering darkness.

The boat capsized and in they went, a tangle of gear and sails and bodies. One head was quickly seen, but although the rescue craft were quickly on the spot only one was hauled into the boat. The rescuers criss-crossed the scene joined by two others from the shore.

'Have you the two of them?' cried Mr Stodart screaming in his fear.

The wind was blowing hard, the tide was on the turn and darkness was closing in. Although the coxswain did not want to mouth the words, he had to shout,

'There's no sign of Scud.'

Chapter 16 Knots!

It was no joke. Boats were everywhere tracking and re-tracing the area around the finish. Men were in the water frantically diving below the surface to seek the missing Scud. Torches lanced the growing gloom but lost power swallowed up in the dark, peaty water. Searching became difficult and fraught.

As the minutes passed the tension grew: They knew they had to find him fast. Dusk brought difficulties untold. Cold and exhaustion were facts they had to face.

On the shore, Fergus thought he heard a cry down from where the boat capsized and sure enough he saw a head.

'Is that you, Fergus? Thank goodness you've come. I'm getting wet. Is Jimmy all right? I thought he must be in trouble – nobody seemed to hear me.'

'Scud, are you all right?' shouted Fergus.

'Did you see that race? We got second. Blew up a bit,'

'But are you fine?'

'Course I am. Just don't want to let go in case the tide carries me further out.'

'Wait till I get a boat down here.'

'What about that run? Did you see it?'

But Fergus was off to get a boat pick up Scud.

'He's here,' he yelled. 'Down here. He's holding on to the boat off the blocks.'

Soon the two were in the shower and even there they could not stop. It was runs and planes and more planes. Everybody else might have been worried, but they had had the time of their lives.

'We didn't do so badly, did we, Fergus? Told you we could sail it. Shouldn't have let the boat get up on end like that though. Ended up in a right bourach.'

'You and Jimmie were great especially on the main. That work was near perfect. Dad'll be pleased. That's what kept you upright.'

'Didn't like the runs, mind,' said Scud. 'In that wind they're dodgy.'

'You kept her straight. That's what counted.'

'What about that?' said Scud. 'That's planing.'

'Jimmie, this guy's doing all the talking. You were brilliant.'

'It was great. It's this guy that's some sailor.'

That night Mrs Stodart was very calm about the whole thing. The sea had always been Scud's second home and something, someone had kept him safe.

Jimmie's Mum and Dad were not upset either. They neither saw it nor understood it. They were proud that their son could sail, but when they heard that he had capsized they were amazed that he was not bothered at all. Scud thought the whole thing was a laugh. Except that he was annoyed at not handling the gust as a sailor should, he did not know what they were all going on about. Next day he was a bit of a hero when the story of his rescue spread. He was better pleased when asked about the planing run they had made. 'Is it true there was only a metre of hull still in the water when you planed?'

'Not quite,' Scud answered keeping the story going. 'We were flying though. The boat took off.' The words spilled out as his heaven seemed to be all around him.

That night though when Fergus got home from school he took one look at Scud recounting his adventures for the umpteenth time and said, 'Knots, it's knots now. Where's the practice rope you were given? I thought you were practising all the time. There's only two days to go before the Cadet competition so get working. We'll check you out at Shore Base tomorrow night. It'll no' be too good for you if you blow it.'

Friday night was a trial for Scud. All the glory of the race had gone as he struggled to get his knots right. One minute he could do it and the next it was all wrong.

'Scud,' said Ann, 'like this. Left over right and right over left and then pull. See, a reef knot. Now do it slowly. I'll take you through it.'

'I know what to do,' shouted Scud.

'Then do it. Just keep saying, left over right, right over left,' said a curiously calm Ann.

'I've got it now,' said a triumphant Scud. He tied it and produced a glorious granny knot.

'It's no good,' said Mairi. I don't know what's wrong, 'Leave it for now. Scud, we'll get Fergus to check you out before you go to the Cadets.'

On Saturday morning they all lined up in their Cadet Division. The Cadet Master said that they had reached the final competition for the divisional championship. After it the Commodore would present the Cadet Trophy to the winning division.

Everyone was ready when the Cadet Master announced that the three divisions would line up in single file in front of a Cadet Mate. They had to tie one of three knots and run to the back of their file. The first division to tie all three knots correctly would be declared the winner.

Scud still couldn't tie knots fast and hadn't even practised the bowline the night before. They would all be standing in line waiting for him to finish – if ever.

It was the bowline first and the three teams progressed steadily down their lines. At first there was nothing in it. Scud was seventh in line.

When his turn came his mind was whirling. What is it you have to say, he muttered. 'A rabbit down a hole, round the rabbit, through the hole, right over left, and round the back. No, that's not right,' he said out loud.

'What are you saying, Scud?' asked Iain who was right behind him.

'I can't remember which way the rabbit goes.'

'It's up the hole, round the back and down the hole again.'

Scud made the hole, but the rabbit didn't seem to want to go in or come out. It was a mess. By the time he reached the mate he did not know where the hole was, never mind the rabbit. The result was a tangle. Twice more he tried, nothing worked. Fergus moved in behind him and said, 'just say it slowly, Scud - up through the hole, round the back and down the hole again. Come on, say it.'

Scud fixed his mind on the words and said slowly and carefully, ‘up through the hole came the rabbit, it went round the back and popped down the hole again.’ His hands just did it. He stared at the knot, threw it at the mate and ran.

But his division was away behind and last after the hold-up. Fergus took over and beat it out. ’Lets – get - moving,’ he murmured, ‘fast-and-sure; - con-cen-trate; - get-it-done.’

Slowly they caught up. Scud shut out his doubts and tied his next two knots without thinking. They were only one behind with three to go but their rivals for the Championship were still leading. Iain was not the fastest but he was never going to get it wrong. Mairi knew what she was doing and Fergus just twisted his wrists and stepped into the lead by a whisker.

They were the Champions.

The Commodore came in, made a little speech and presented the trophy for the Best Cadet Division to Fergus as Leading Hand. Scud had tears in his eyes – he was a real softy sometimes – but he and Jimmie were soon singing, ‘We are the ‘Goldies’ to a tune no one else had ever heard of.

Fergus stepped up to stop them, but Mairi whispered, ’leave them. Let them work off steam. They’ve had a hard week.’

They met at Shore Base on Sunday and lay about as if that was it. They were getting results when they sailed as the Ospreys and now as part of a division at the Cadets they had won the Divisional Championship. They were a bit exhausted, but they felt like they had done it all. Life was great. But Mairi, as usual, took things in hand. ‘Come on then, that’s all past. The big one is still to come. If you think the cadet fight was tough, wait till you go to the Schools.’

‘You‘re right,’ said Fergus. ‘Nigel Fairfell was there before he left school and it was rough. He knows a few of this year’s sailors. Thinks two of the boats are the big favourites.’

‘It’s all in Mirrors, isn’t it?’ said Ann.

‘Yeah,’ said Fergus. ‘We’ll have to borrow. I think every school can enter three boats but maybe it’s two. You’ve got to be entered by the school.’

Iain and Pete quickly said they wouldn't apply but would be reserves and back-up. You need back-up at a thing like this.

'Course the school might enter someone else,' said Mairi.

'Away you go,' said Ann. 'Who's going to beat us?

'Duncan McNight? He's no mug,' said Mairi.

'We'll see,' said Fergus, 'but we'll have to practise in Mirrors. It means staying out of "Osprey" for a bit, but that will give Iain and Pete a chance to sail it.'

'Which boats are we going to use?' asked Scud.

'Well, Nigel will lend us his until the championships. He'll coach us and the Roxburgh boys will help as well.'

'The Roxburgh boys! I thought you said they were idiots,' said Scud.'

'Oh Scud, wise up. I didn't mean they were actually idiots. They're great. They've won everything. It's just that if you keep thinking they're great, you'll never beat them.'

'What about a second boat?' said Ann. 'I mean a good one.'

'Well, believe it or not, Mr Roxburgh still has their old championship boat. I think we can have it. It hasn't been sailed for a while so we'll have to do it up, but it is a good one.'

'Brilliant,' said Ann. 'We can do it up when the holidays start as long as we can practise in it now.'

'And here's the really good bit. Mr Roxburgh might let the Ospreys sail it all the time.'

'Will he,' said Mairi. 'There's our second boat then.'

'Well, it's not definite. He just said that the Ospreys need another boat and his "Agamemnon" might just be the thing.'

'I knew he was pleased that Scud took Jimmie as crew the other night,' said Mairi.

'We'll see,' said Fergus.

'What about the two boats you were talking about, Fergus,' said Scud, in the "Schools".

''Oh, they're good and they're tough. We'll be up against it, Scud.'

Chapter 17 This is tough, Scud.

The challenge was on.

'They're tough. What do you mean?' asked Scud a little belligerently.

'Hell,' said Fergus, 'some of them do more than sail against you. Nigel says they fight you.'

'Fight you – hit you, you mean?'

'Not with their fists but with everything else. The rule book, sarcasm, trying to ruin your confidence and sometimes a bit more. We'll have to stand up to it. Nigel was probably thinking about one particular boat but he said it was like a football game without a referee in the middle.'

'Who are the two Nigel thinks are the main opposition?' said Mairi.

'Well, there is a brother and sister team,' said Fergus. 'They're good. They won last year and they will take some beating.'

'What are they called,' said Ann, 'so that we'll know them.'

'They're the Drummonds. Nigel will tell us about them. The other danger boat is the rough one. They are not really Mirror sailors at all and Nigel says they're too heavy for the boat, but they are experienced racers.'

'Oh! Forget them. What about our own arrangements?' said Mairi.

'Will we get the Roxburgh boat for you? Training then on the water with Nigel or the Roxburgh boys would be a good idea. What do you think?' said Fergus.

'I fancy that. I'll go and see Mr. Roxburgh to-night,' said Mairi, 'and then we'll sail and sail and sail. We'll do all the club races in Mirrors and now that the exams are over we can practise against each other at night. The six of us can go out.'

That was settled and they started the next night by taking the "Agememnon" up to the Stodart garage. It was maybe a little worn but there was nothing seriously wrong. Everything was checked by

Mr Roxburgh and he took pains to explain the working of the spinnaker to Mairi and Ann.

They decided to start with the Wednesday race and it was quite an occasion. It was the first time the six Ospreys had raced together. Fergus and Scud won the race for Mirrors, Jenny and Ann got a fourth but it was their first race in the new Mirror and Pete and Iain were third in the mid-week points' series.

It was a good race for them all.

That night Fergus mentioned that their campaign for the "Schools" had begun.

'What! I thought I said I wanted to know about this kind of trip,' Mum said angrily.

'Nothing's been arranged, Mum. We have to be picked by the school before that, but we have to practise. If we are picked we want the two of you to come and support us.'

On the Saturday, Nigel crewed for Fergus and Hugh Roxburgh crewed for Mairi in the club race and would you believe it they were first and second. After the race finished Scud and Ann went out and Nigel and the other Roxburgh brother Jim put them through it as crews.

Scud could feel enthusiasm rising in him. It might have been nerves but he didn't care. When he came ashore he was bubbling over. 'When we can sail like that, we'll win the "Schools".'

'He checked all my movements. I had to be so exact. "You look like a dancer", he said, "be like one". He kept calling out the time when we went about. I can't wait for it. We'll murder them.'

That night after Mr. Stodart saw what was happening he took Fergus aside and had a word. 'This is a big thing you are going in for. I think we better help this time.'

'I hoped you might offer, Dad. I knew you would. We're not picked yet for the school team, but if we are, could you organise the transport?'

'Have you got road trailers for the two boats?'

'Yes, they come with the boats. They're combis, you know combination launchers and trailers.'

'Right, I'll take that over and see if Mr Hargreaves will help. I'll have a word.'

'Now about Scud. He's good, he is very good, but he's young for this kind of thing. If anything he is too keen. Gets worked up. You will have to look after him especially in the weeks before the championship. The tension is mounting already. I even heard them arguing about it in the club last night. Try not to talk about it all the time.'

'I know, Dad. I've always got to keep him on an even keel but it's these stories he tells. He's got something but I never know what to believe.'

'He just has a vivid imagination, that's all.'

'But the things he seems to know about. Where does he get it all? A lot of it's true. The only thing I can think of is to get him doing other things as well.'

'That's good. He'll settle down. Just keep him as calm as possible. Anyway, I'll do the transport.'

The Ospreys met at Shore Base on Sunday. All the talk was about the training sessions with Nigel and the Roxburgh boys until Pete said, 'we met Mr Turner in the village this morning.'

'He was in the village on a Sunday morning?' said Ann.

'Yes, that's what I'm saying and what he told us is important. There is a letter in the post but he told us what was in it. The coin has sold for £160.'

The noise nearly raised the roof.

'That's a new spinnaker for sure,' said Iain.

'And,' said Pete, as he tried to get a word in, 'they have identified the piece of metal as the same metal that Andrea de Ferrara used for his famous swords and daggers.'

'Does that make it more valuable?' said Mairi.

'No, it's not worth much but it is interesting. Some people think that Ferrara was Andrew Ferrier of Arbroath and finding it here in another old fishing village says something about that story.'

'Anyway they are going to do more work on it and they will tell us about it.'

'But the spinnaker, can we buy one now?' said Mairi.

'We'll have a £160 probably by tomorrow,' said Pete.

'Fergus,' said Mairi, 'will you get the prices and work out which one we should get for "Osprey".'

'Sure, I'll see about it next week.'

'Okay then,' said Mairi.' Things seem to be going fine. Same crew list for next week, Fergus?'

'Yeah, but we better start practising with the spinnakers. Not in a race but on the water – get the movements right. We'll have spinnakers for the Mirrors and when the new one for "Osprey" comes, you too, Pete and Iain.'

'When is the "Schools" anyway?' said Pete.

'It's the third weekend in August. The last week of the holidays,' said Fergus. 'We'll have the whole of the holidays to practise.'

'It's a funny time to be having a school's event. The school will be closed,' said Mairi.

'I know but the school enters the team before the end of term and it's up to the club running the event.'

'How many boats are there likely to be?' said Pete.

'There were thirty-one last year and they say there will be more this time.'

'It's some event,' said Mairi. 'I hope we're ready for it.'

'We're coming on and after a summer with our coaches we'll be ready,' said Fergus.

'We'll win,' murmured Scud.

Chapter 18 Pressure

The pace heated up.

Fergus and Scud; Mairi and Ann; and Duncan McNight and his crew, William Carlyle, were picked for the school.

There was a panic over Scud: Some said that because he attended the local primary he was not at the same school as Fergus. Unfortunately Scud found out and blew his top. I'm going whether they like it or not.'

'Don't worry, Scud. It'll all get fixed up. You'll see.'

'I know. I don't know what I'm worrying about. Christiana says I'm good enough and I'll be there.'

'Course you are. You'll prove it in the crew's race.'

'The crew's race?'

'The crew takes the helm in the third race.'

Ann, who was standing listening to Fergus, screamed.

'I'm to helm at the "Schools" I've hardly ever helmed and never with thirty boats.' It was unlike Ann to be scared of competition, but this was a big event and the pressure was beginning to get to her.

'You think I'm good enough, Fergus, don't you,' said Scud.

'Yes I do but before the two of you get too excited, it doesn't count for the main event. It's on its own for a medal. Anyway Scud, you can always get one of these dead people you're always talking to, to help. If you get into trouble I'll be in the boat as your crew and if Christiana is there as well, so much the better.'

Ann immediately wanted to go and practise helming but Scud was standing there bemused until he suddenly rushed over to Ann to shake her hand. 'We're both going to be helming at the "Schools" and if anybody thinks I'm not going they better think again.'

Next day the Headmaster sent for Fergus. 'This business of your crew for the sailing championship: Just to say that I do not know what all the fuss is about. Technically the Primary is part of this school so there is no problem. Why they did not ask me about it I do not know.'

Scud just grinned when he heard and said, 'Thanks Fergus.'

The two crews raced every Wednesday and at the weekend. They went out regularly on non-racing days and practised against each other. They went round buoys until it became a kind of rhythmic movement – poetry in motion - and slowly improved their boat speed by sailing alongside each other.

Sitting down in Shore Base the Ospreys gave a lot of thought to the pressure the opposition would put them under. 'Nigel says it's called "psyching up",' said Fergus. 'They try to get you worked up using fancy sailing words and what they did at the last regatta. They get dressed up in matching sailing gear: They look good and you are meant to believe that they are good.'

'You mean we're going to get dressed up in Osprey colours.' said Scud.

'No we are not,' said Mairi. 'We'll be spending our money on the boat and we'll win by being good.'

'Yes,' said Fergus 'but we'll be doing a few things of our own. It's called, "batting the ba' back". Some of them will think we're just country hicks. They'll learn. I've been talking to one of the Roxburgh boys and he's given me one or two ideas.'

'What?' said Scud.

'Just wait, and see. And we're not going to mix much. We'll go into our shell where they can't affect us.'

'You got that, Scud?' said Mairi. 'Mind you, you'd probably affect them.'

The Ospreys had one big test before the "Schools". The Club held a week long regatta and sailors came from all over. The "Schools" pair stayed in Mirrors and Pete and Iain used the "Osprey".

The two Mirrors were overwhelmed on the first day, but Fergus and Scud got a second on the last day which brought them up to third in the series. Mairi and Ann sailed steadily but were not as good and ended up seventh. Pete and Iain got a prize: they were fourth in the slow handicap. Because there were more boats in the handicap four awards were made. You should have heard the cheers when they went up for their prizes.

When they came back to the group, Scud shook hands and said, ‘You said to look out when you got going.’

The weeks passed by and final arrangements were made. The Ospreys worked on the two Mirrors. Agamemnon’s hull was rubbed and painted until it was beautifully smooth. The two boats looked what they were: two championship racing boats.

At the last moment, Duncan McNight had to call off – chicken pox.

The day dawned and the convoy set out for the “Schools”. It was exciting, but Fergus had warned everybody to be very controlled from the minute they left the village. ‘Just be natural,’ he said. ’If you see something interesting tell the rest of us about it. They did all this, played games and enjoyed themselves.

Eventually they arrived at a scene like a carnival. There were boats everywhere with colourful red sails. People were pulling sails up and down, testing, checking and experimenting. They were all on dry land, a great, fluttering red blob set against the green of the dingy park.

Flags were flying around the park and the club and there was even a van selling ice cream. People were walking about looking at the boats and buying things from the local chandler’s van.

They stopped in front of the club and went in to register. There was a big table with papers and stickers and things to sign.

‘New arrivals?’ said the man behind the table. ‘Great to see you, where are you from?’ When he was told he said, ’you’ve come a long way. I think you are the first we’ve ever had from away over there.’

They were allocated two spaces in the park, collected their copies of the racing instructions, found out where their hotel was and went out again.

‘He made it sound as if we come from Timbuktu,’ said Ann. ‘I expect he thinks we race in dugout canoes.’

But everyone kept quiet. They just looked around and took it all in. They found their spaces, unloaded the boats and started to lay out their gear. They did not attract much attention at first but soon a little crowd gathered around.

‘First time here then? Haven’t seen you lot before,’ somebody said. Everybody seemed to know everybody else and they were full of themselves.

‘What club are you in?’ they were asked.

‘I know,’ shouted a lad in a bright purple sailing suit. It’s the Paddling Pool Racers. You’re racers then. That’ll be good,’ he giggled to great laughter from the crowd.

The Ospreys kept quiet and carried on setting things up. When everything was out including all the extra equipment that Fergus had brought, the taunts gradually died down.

‘Look at their jammers. They’re Harkens.’ The crowd around the boats were impressed and so they should have been. The two Mirrors were championship boats. They had been sailed by Nigel and the Roxburgh boys at championships all over Great Britain. The crowd recognised quality and started to wonder. Who were these people?

Fergus sensed that things were going well and murmured to the others, ‘keep going, we’ve got them wondering.’

There was no time to go for a sail, but the racing started next day with a practice race. Mr Stodart and Mr Hargreaves came back after visiting the club and said it was time to go to the hotel.

‘Everything ready then? Everything out of the cars? Got all your gear?’ Just do a last check before we put on the covers.’

Things seemed fine. Pete grabbed a cover and was hauling it on when Scud said quietly, ‘Fergus have you got our jib?’

‘It’s rolled up with the main.’

‘No, it isn’t,’ said Scud. ‘Look, it isn’t there.’

‘They feverishly searched all over, in the cars, in the boats, on the ground. It wasn’t anywhere.’

They had left their jib at home.

Chapter 19 "The Schools"

Disaster threatened.

'We'll easily borrow one,' said Mr Hargreaves. 'I'll go up to the clubhouse now and see what I can do.'

'Yes, but that's no good,' wailed Scud. 'It's Nigel's new jib.'

'He means we'll never borrow a jib as good as Nigel's,' said Fergus. 'It's got the new wire luff.'

Everyone looked at each other. Mr. Stodart smiled uncomfortably and said, 'I'll go back for it.'

'No, Dad,' said Fergus. 'We want it but it's too far. It'd be about 300 miles there and back.'

There was a look of fanaticism in Scud's eyes and Mr Stodart had seen it.

'No, I'll go. Where is it?'

'It must be lying in the porch. They were both there.'

'Right. I'll be back in plenty time for the practice race.'

'I'll come too,' said Mr Hargreaves, 'and share the driving. Can you lot get back to the hotel?'

There they left it and the Ospreys settled down to wait.

'We're not sitting up all night,' said Mairi. 'It'll do no good if we're too tired to race tomorrow. The Dads won't thank us for that.'

Everyone did sleep and did not even hear the two Dads come in early next morning.

They all met at breakfast and before anybody could say anything, Mr Stodart looked at Scud, grimaced and said, 'It's in our room. You'd better win.'

'We will, we will,' said Scud.

'Not necessarily to-day though,' said Mr Stodart. 'These inland lochs are funny places. The wind goes all over the place so use the practice race to get to know the water. Spend more time examining the sailing area than trying to beat the opposition. Let them do what ever they want. Make your mistakes to-day.'

The race practice did not start until two o'clock so they spent the time doing all the mysterious things sailors do to their boats both off and on the water. Mr Stodart spoke to Fergus on the quiet.

'Remember Fergus, look after your young brother. This is a huge thing for him.'

'I will but I'm no' sure he needs looking after. The things he knows. He seems to believe that his ancestors are looking after him. I can't make head or tail of it but there's something in it.'

'It's just his confidence,' said Mr Stodart 'and that is a good thing. Just help him to keep it.'

At race time Fergus and Mairi went out to the line and tried out several starting positions. Seeing them go all over the place, one "heid banger", as such people were known at home, had to shout, 'Lost are you? London's that way.' But the Ospreys ignored him and got ready for the first counting race next day.

'Did you notice the wind coming off that hill?' said Fergus to Mairi. 'It bends round when you get near it. Watch for it straightening out the beat if it's like that tomorrow.'

'A starboard start would have been best today, wouldn't it,' said Mairi, 'if it wasn't so shallow over there.'

'Yeah, it's a risk but I'll need to think about it.'

'Take it,' said Scud. 'It'll be fine.'

'Oh yeah!' said Fergus.

Scud just shrugged.

'Scud, it's not fairy land time. Sounds like one of your stories.'

'No, Fergus. I got told.'

'Well never mind all that. If I take it you'll have to be fast on the board. Have you got that, Scud? Your girl friend can be there as well as far as I'm concerned, but if I take that side make sure the board doesn't strike. It'll be a beat.'

The first counting race of four started next morning and the Ospreys were ready. The attention was on the Drummonds and the "Roughies" and you would not believe what happened.

There were forty-three boats competing and forty-one were clustered round the port hand end. The two favourites had decided to start there and everybody except the Ospreys had followed them. Mairi went for the middle of the line but Fergus and Scud were at the starboard end on their own. It looked odd.

After the five minute gun had gone two of the helpers went over to Fergus in one of the safety boats and said, 'You are at the wrong end. You shouldn't start here.'

'Why not?' said Fergus.

'It's the wrong end.'

'Why?'

The two didn't seem to know. It was a test of confidence for Fergus but he stayed where he was. He thought the starting line was squint – biased sailors call it – and that the starboard end would give them an advantage.

When the starting gun fired Fergus and Scud got clean away and beat the Drummonds to the first mark by twenty metres. The "Roughies were third and there in fourth were Mairi and Ann.

Try as they might nobody could get near Fergus and Scud. The advantage of the excellent start left them in a commanding position. They sailed in undisturbed air which filled their sails beautifully. They romped away with the first race.

Mairi and Ann lost another place but were delighted with their fifth.

At lunch time, people had a good look at the Osprey boats. There was not much said but it was obvious that a great deal of re-thinking was going on.

The Drummonds came over and said hello. 'We haven't met before. You sail out west do you?' They were very friendly but the Ospreys didn't say much.

The second race was different. Fergus and Scud were attacked from the word go. The wind conditions were exactly the same and although the Race Officer had removed the line bias Fergus picked the starboard end again. There were a few boats strung along the line but most were still at the other end.

The "Roughies" were a problem now and they came down the line to deal with this upstart boat. They kept abreast and tried to force Fergus off the end of the line beyond the buoy but plans and know how (Willie Black's advice for this kind of thing) kept him in control. He had no intention of starting at the buoy. Twenty seconds before the start Fergus came off the wind, swung round their transom, sailed ten yards down a line quite clear of other boats and came up tight to cross the line just as the gun boomed out.

The "Roughies" vented all the fury they possessed. They swung round and sailed straight for our pair screaming "starboard" and demanding right of way. But both boats were on the starboard tack and they had no prior rights. As it turned out they missed the Osprey's stern and Fergus sailed clean away.

The Drummonds had made a clever start. They placed themselves in the middle of the line to keep Fergus under control. When the two boats tacked the Drummonds were clear in front and so it stayed until they reached the buoy.

Mairi and Ann were in the wars. Stuck in a mess of boats and blanked off from the wind they could not find an escape. When shouts and calls and frantic moves seemed to clear a way the "Roughies" took their revenge. Every move to use the speed and freedom of the windward side was blocked.

'Can't you do anything about this?' shouted an exasperated Ann.

'Not a lot at the moment,' said Mairi. 'But I'll solve it. I'll tack out of it in a minute. They're not doing themselves any good.'

'Keep sailing. They're just being rotten. It's keeping them back as well. They'll get fed up covering us.'

Meantime, Fergus and Scud were trying to get in front of the Drummond boat. Every move was countered until the second beat. The Drummonds went to port but Fergus left the mark to starboard. Their opponents immediately gained.'

'You've picked the wrong side,' said Scud.

'Quiet. Concentrate. You'll see.'

Fergus made straight for the hill on the right hand side of the course. He certainly fell back at first but as soon as the hill bent the wind he could sail much closer to the mark. Suddenly, he had narrowed the angle and had a much shorter distance to sail than the

Drummonds. He was round a good twenty metres in front and never lost it.

Mairi was much further back this time. The nonsense with the "Roughies" had ruined her race. She and Ann were twenty-fifth.

The "Roughies" came off in a furious mood and instantly lodged a protest against Fergus and Scud.

'What do we do now?' asked a worried Scud.

Mr Stodart explained. 'It is like a court. They go in and make their case. Then you get to tell your side of it. You'll be questioned.'

'But we haven't done anything,' said Scud.

'I know,' said Mr Stodart. 'They are just trying to make you lose a good result.'

The protest meeting heard Fergus' description of the start and then re-questioned the "Roughies" skipper. He said again that Fergus had gone right across their bow at right angles and they had just missed them.

The Chairman then said, 'I believe they got a good start. Is that correct?'

'Yes and it's not fair. They ruined ours.' said the crew of the "Roughies".'

'So they were sailing in the right direction for a good start. If you were sailing at right angles to their boat you must have been well off course.'

Silence reigned: The "Roughies" had fallen into their own hole.

'Both boats were on starboard,' said the Chairman, 'but you were not on a correct course. Case dismissed – not sailing a true course.'

'I didn't like that much,' said Scud still in a state of shock.

'Never mind, that's two wins,' said Mairi. 'Your turn now unless Ann beats you.'

And Scud at ten years old won the crew's race at the "Schools".

First of all he had a great start. The line went ever so squint again and Fergus advised him to start at the starboard end.

The "Roughies" had worked it out as well and had come down to play their usual games. Fergus kept cool and told Scud to keep back until the last possible moment. With twenty seconds to go Fergus called and Scud dived into the position next to the buoy. So did the "Roughies".'

When the two boats darted towards the one space the "Roughies" ran aground. They were a lot heavier than the Ospreys and had forgotten about the shallow water. Fergus hadn't.

Scud roared, 'They're stuck!'

He didn't look back then or throughout the race. It was a repeat of the first and with Fergus making him sail a sensible no mistakes race he won.

But that night was a near disaster. Oh they were happy. They were nearly delirious and discipline collapsed. It was 'Did you see that?' and 'That was some start.'

In spite of it all Mairi felt something wasn't quite right but could not work out what was wrong.

Ann was pleased with their tenth. All the hard work was paying off and she had enjoyed her race as a helm, but when she and Mairi were alone with tears in her eyes she said, 'I have to tell you something. It's not the right time but I have to tell somebody. It's killing me.'

'Yeah, I thought there was something. What is it?'

'I'm leaving the Ospreys. So is Iain.'

'What!'

'After the "Schools", I can't crew for you any more.'

'But what's wrong?'

'My Dad's been posted. He's going to another aerodrome and we've got to leave. I didn't mean to tell you until after the Championships but I had to say something. I don't know if my Dad has said anything.'

'When are you going?'

'He's going next week and we will follow almost right after. Don't tell anyone else until this is over. We've got this to finish and that lot are not going to sail on top of us again.' Tears gone, Ann gritted her teeth and shouted, 'Right.'

'Right,' said Mairi. We'll give them hell tomorrow.'

'Eventually they all got to sleep but they were a sorry looking bunch in the morning. Fergus and Scud only needed one more win and they could not lose.

They got off to a good start – second boat away. The Drummonds as usual were first. The "Roughies" were third. Marie and Ann put the bad news behind them and nobody noticed – they all looked bad. They got off seventh and were well pleased.

The race was a battle. It was windy, water was smashing into the boat and the heavier crews had an advantage. The lead changed hands several times with the big three in and out of the lead.

And then disaster struck. Coming off the run on to the beat Fergus and Scud took the full force of the gale as they pulled in the sails on the turn. It was if a giant hand had swept the boat from bow to stern. Everything went overboard, the mast, both sails and all the rigging. Fergus and Scud were left floating amongst the wreckage. The shackle pin on the starboard shroud had come out and that was enough to lose everything. Was it not tightened? Was this the result of their sleepless night?

The Drummonds beat the "Roughies" over the line and Mairi and Ann got a wonderful fifth. It still left Fergus and Scud in good position but if the Drummonds won the last race they could win on count-back.

The last race was at 2 o'clock and you can be sure that the boats were checked thoroughly this time. They discussed their position and went over possible tactics again,

' Wherever you end up, Fergus,' said Mr Stodart, 'you have got to beat the Drummonds. If they win that will see them home.'

As it turned out all the excitement was with Mairi and Ann. They were buffeted from start to the finish. One boat got inside them at the first mark and they had to go wide. For some reason it did not turn round the buoy but kept straight on and nearly forced Mairi and Ann on to the shore. At another mark about five boats were crowded up side by side all demanding right of way and shouting for water rights. Mairi and Ann were inside boat but nobody would listen and nobody would give them room to get round. Ann was furious and shouting her head off with cries of 'water' interspersed with 'get your flaming boat out the way.' Suddenly, her birth mark glowing red and angry as only Ann could be, for some reason she shouted 'Knickers'.

Would you believe it, all the boats sheared off and the Ospreys got round and away. Ann looked at Mairi and smiled, 'Men', she said. But it was tight all the way round and they had to be content with a tenth.

By contrast Fergus and Scud had a beautiful race. They started first but with the Drummonds in close contention. The two boats fought each other inch by inch but Fergus and Scud were not to be denied.

They were at their magnificent best and nothing fazed them. Like a well oiled machine, they beat, they reached, and they ran. They met the Drummonds' every challenge and claimed the title with every move they made.

They crossed the line a full five metres out in front and people said they had never seen a better championship team and never once a better race to decide the honours. The cheers rang out and they later took their due. A shield to show that they had won, a token to record they had achieved their goal.

The other four took no less pride in such a feat for they were Ospreys too.

THE CALL OF THE HELIX

PART THREE

THE DOUBLE HELIX

'Tis but an Avenue

The Sennachie of the Ri,
The High Kings of
The Western Seas.

Chapter 20 Who is this Christiana?

They were champions now.

Everybody wanted to shake hands. Six of them – Fergus made sure of that. They were not unknown any more but as The Osprey, the champions of all the schools.

Even when they arrived home the village had turned out to welcome them. Somebody had organised a farm trailer to drive them around the streets. By the time they actually got home they were exhausted and Mairi took over.

'I've lost it,' she said. 'I'm going to bed. Two o'clock tomorrow. Shore Base. Okay?'

They all sat down in Shore Base next day and looked at each other. They were washed out, sailed out and limp.

'I don't know how we did it,' said Mairi. 'I suppose we're not dreaming, are we. It doesn't seem real.'

'Scud might be,' said Fergus, 'but the Ospreys did win it and you, Mairi, Ann were fifth out of forty-three boats and the Ospreys have still got Iain and Pete coming up.

For the moment everyone had forgotten that Ann and Iain were leaving. They had been told but yesterday was not a day to dwell on that.

'It's a miracle,' said Ann.

'It was good sailing,' said Fergus 'in spite of Scud's girl friend being in the boat with us.'

'What!' said Ann.

'So he says.'

'No I didn't,' said Scud. 'I said she told me it would be all right to use the shallow end of the line.'

'Never mind,' said Mairi. 'If Scud says she's a friend of ours that's fine. However, I know we are a bit past it at the moment, but when we recover we've got to work out what we do next. We'll have a good rest and then think about it.'

That very next morning Scud woke up Fergus. 'She's been. She wanted to tell me about treasure, well, rings, two golden rings twisted together – she calls them the "Double Helix". She's got to find them.'

'Come on, Fergus,' shouted Scud. 'Wake up. She needs our help. It's important and it has taken her a long time to trace them.'

'Scud,' said a bleary eyed Fergus struggling to waken up. 'This is no' real. What are you talking about?' Who needs our help?'

'Christiana, my friend, Angus Og's cousin. The one who told me there was treasure in the ice-house. The rings! The rings are somewhere in a forest up here.'

'Scud, start again, what rings?'

'The rings she calls the Double Helix that's guarded by two golden eagles.'

'Oh yeah, you said that. Golden eagles, are you sure?'

'Yes, I don't know where but Christiana thinks it might be on the edge of a forest.'

There was a forest on the other side of the bay and two up the river. And right across the firth there was a huge one.

'Is that all she knows,' said Fergus. 'It's no' much.'

'No, but being on the edge of a forest will help.'

'Why doesn't she get it herself? She seems to be good at whizzing all over the place.'

'She can't do that,'

'Why did I know that would be the answer?'

'Magic people can't do that kind of thing. They know a lot and they can make things happen, but they can't do it themselves.'

'So you're saying she's magic.'

'No, well, yes. She's not a wizard or anything, but she lived 700 years ago so she must be something like that.'

'So we go looking for a nest with two rings in it that are stuck together. How do we know the right nest?'

'The eagles are special. They've got two gold coloured circles on their legs. You know, on the feathers they have on their legs. They look like trousers.'

'And the rings, what's so special about them?'

'They're important. She wants them awful bad.'

'Okay, but this better be true.'

'I'm telling you. We've got to do something.'

'We'll talk about it with Mairi and Pete and we'll have to know who this Christiana is or who she was. The whole thing baffles me.'

'But we will help, won't we Ferry? We've got to help.'

'For a start, stop calling me Ferry. For another, go and find Mairi and Pete. We're meeting here at 12 o'clock. They're in this too.'

'Right,' said Fergus when they were all together. 'You've all heard of Scud's friend, Christiana – the one who was born 700 years ago. Now she wants him to find two golden rings that are twisted together. – that makes them a "Double Helix" apparently.'

'What's a Double Helix?' said Pete baffled for once.

'I don't know,' said Fergus. 'I thought you would.'

'I know,' said Mairi. 'It's what makes you what you are. You know genes and all that.'

'I hope this is not magic again, Scud,' said Fergus.

'Maybe it is.' said Scud. 'I don't know.'

'Well anyway,' said Fergus. 'I reckon it has to be the four of us or none of us. It can't be Ann or Iain. They'll be away by next week. I'll go over everything I know and then you can question Scud.'

When Fergus finished, Mairi said, 'This is all true, is it, Scud?'

'Yes, I'm telling you. These things happen.'

'I know,' said Mairi 'and if we find the rings that will prove it.'

'You're in then?' said Fergus.

'Oh yes, got to be.'

'And you, Pete?'

'Oh yeah, I'm in.'

'Right,' said Fergus. 'Well I must admit something is happening. I don't know what but we better try and find out.

For a start - who is this Christiana exactly? '

Chapter 21 A Celtic Princess

'She's a princess,' said Scud. 'A sailing princess.'

'She's the head of her Clan. She has sailed all her life and she's good. I think she's quite young and she is a girl.'

'For god's sake,' exploded Fergus. 'Of course she's a girl, but how she is young after 700 years beats me.'

'Fergus,' said Mairi. 'Cool it. He's doing his best so shut up until we hear what he does know. Scud, carry on.'

'What I mean is that not many girls got to sail in her time. And another thing, her father made her his heir to become the Chief after him. That didn't happen much either. She needs the two gold rings to prove to her brothers that she is the rightful Chieftain. All I know is that her granduncle Dugal gave them away to the monks at Durham Abbey and there was trouble about who was the correct King or Queen.'

'But how did the eagles get them,' said Pete.

'Well, Durham were asked for the rings back, but the Abbot wouldn't return them. It was awkward to do anything about it because they were holy men and you couldn't fight them.

'So a plan was worked out. Two eagles, big, fierce eagles, were taught to do the job. First it was hunting foxes and then bright objects until they only picked up certain gold objects. The King was probably Christiana's father, knew that when the Abbey had an outdoor festival they would be on display and he would be near with his eagles.'

'Okay then, so he got them,' said Fergus. 'Why are we looking for them?'

'He didn't get them. He forgot that his eagles were male and female and for once they didn't return to him. They were ready to mate so they flew somewhere, built a nest and reared two eaglets. The rings fell into the nest and she thinks they are still there.'

'What!' said Fergus, 'for seven hundred years?'

‘Think so. Nobody has had them since then and it has caused a lot of bother. If Christiana had them there wouldn’t be any argument about her being chief.’

Nobody said anything. It was some story. Scud believed it, but the others did not know what to think.

‘Eventually,’ Mairi said, ‘Either we help or we don’t. If we find the rings in an eagle’s nest, it must be true.’

‘And Fergus,’ said Mairi, ‘we have two good clues. Christiana seems sure the nest is at the edge of a forest up here and there can’t be many eagles with gold ring markings on their legs.’

Yeah,’ said Fergus. ‘I don’t know what is happening but you’re right. It is affecting our sailing so we’d better get it sorted out. ‘

‘Okay,’ said Mairi. ‘Let’s go for it. We’ll plan expeditions and you, Fergus. will have to be the leader. There will be a lot of sailing and we’ll need something bigger than our racing boats. We can do the local forests at weekends, but the big one on the other side of the Firth will have to be on the school holidays.’

‘What about Christiana?’ said Fergus. ‘Is she coming?’

‘I’m not sure,’ said Scud. ‘I’ll ask her next time.’

‘Okay,’ said Fergus, ‘but she should be there – it’s for her benefit. Finding the rings will prove something. I’ll organise the sailing. Mairi, you plan the journeys; and Pete, you’re in charge of equipment. Get us something like a Wayfarer. Scud, reach Christiana. We need a lot more information.’

‘But remember,’ he said, ‘we’re racing on Saturday.’

Chapter 22 The Clash

It was Scud against Fergus.

Both Osprey crews were sailing Mirror dinghies with Scud helming and Mairi crewing for him. Pete was keen to crew for Fergus because they got on well and Fergus was a good sailor.

Fergus had taught his youngest brother a lot of things but Scud was a born sailor and it was time he struck out on his own. It would be the first time racing against each other.

'It's a big day on Saturday,' said Fergus. 'You up for it?'

'I think so but it will be strange fighting each other.'

Fergus liked his younger brother and Scud worshipped Fergus. Scud's stories could irritate Fergus but he simply tried to keep him in check for his own sake.

On Saturday morning the four of them arrived at the dinghy park but separated to get their own boat ready. Scud had an advantage having Mairi as crew. She was a skipper in her own right and it showed. She could make other sailors sit up and take notice. But Mairi also knew that Scud had something the others did not have – the ability to be a world beater. She did not know what it was that made him so, but she wanted him to reach that peak - and she liked him too.

Fergus and Pete followed them out to the starting line and the two of them began to prepare their moves. This Saturday the line was squint and it was important to notice it. Scud looked at Mairi and Fergus spoke to Pete and they looked at each other. The fight was on. Who was going to get the favoured place next to the buoy?

With 10 seconds to go Scud made straight for the good end, but left a little gap between him and the buoy and stayed slightly off the wind.

At five seconds – it all happened in a flash – with Scud in second position and Fergus alongside him but a little way behind, Scud shouted 'up-up-up'.

Mairi hauled in her sail in time with Scud's main sail and the boat was forced up to the wind and the buoy. By the rules Fergus had to move up wind, was forced to the wrong side of the buoy and failed to cross the line. Scud was off.

Fergus shouted, 'Yah Devil.' He had underestimated his young brother although he had taught him that manoeuvre the year before.

It put Scud and Mairi away ahead of everybody and they never lost that place. The first race between Scud and Fergus was won by Scud and back at the dinghy park he and Mairi had grins from ear to ear.

'I know, I know, you wait,' said Fergus.

'It was a great start for us anyway,' said Mairi 'but what about this stronger boat you're looking for Pete. Seen anything?'

'There's the old clinker job down at the pier,' said Pete. 'Don't know what kind it is, but that hull will take some bashing.'

'Whose is it?' said Mairi.

'It's a club boat,' said Fergus. 'Check it, Pete. They'll lend us it if we do it up.'

Pete reported it sound but needing a thorough check to make sure everything worked. 'It'll leak,' he said. 'We'll need to sink it to let the hull swell again. It's been lying in the sun and the planks have shrunk. Won't take long.'

The four of them hauled the club's 16 footer out of the water after two day's submersion, but it was hard work.

'Is Christiana going to help or not?' said Fergus. 'That's the worst of these magic folk. They're never around when you need them.'

'How does it look, Pete?' said Mairi.

'Fine. It's taken up a treat. The planks are tight. She'll be fine.'

'That's great,' said Fergus. 'We'll work on her and then I think we should go next weekend. There's no racing so we're missing nothing and could start with the forest up river at Dunsire. It isn't big; we'll do it in a weekend. What do you think?'

'Right,' said Mairi. 'Agreed? We've got the gear but what about food?'

Silence ruled until Mairi said, 'all right Fergus I'll do it, but I don't know why it should always be me. The leader is allowed to cook, you know.'

'Aw Mairi, you're good at it,' said Fergus, 'but I tell you what, maybe Christiana is good at it.'

They never found out but all of a sudden they all thought she was near or that something odd was happening. It was Scud who first felt it.

'Mairi, do you feel anything?' he said.

'Yes, I've gone all cold.'

'Suddenly, all four were scared. Black cloud rolled in from the south west, the wind started to burst through in gusts and jagged streaks of rain tore into them.

'We're being attacked. No it's Christiana, she's being attacked. I can feel it, Ferry,' Scud shouted. 'Help her!'

'Where is she? Quick' said Fergus running on to the beach. 'I still can't see her. Where is she? What are you talking about, Scud?'

Only Scud knew what was happening.

Christiana was trapped: At the entrance to her own sea-loch at Moidart with her Castle of Tioram high on the height, two longships with oars beating in lashing arcs, were attacking her craft.

Up on her sailing platform Christiana took in the danger. The boats barred her passage to the sea. Immediately, she charged slightly to the right of the left hand boat, pushed the rudder hard away from her and bore down on her other foe. 'Now,' she cried and all her right hand oars were raised as she made a searing, tearing run down her enemy's side to shatter oars and toss oarsmen into scrap.

As the advantage swung to her the smaller of the two invaders chose to run leaving her mistress of her seas. The clouds cleared, the wind and rain petered out and the air was warm again.

Scud stopped, looked up and said,'It's over. She's all right.'

'I'm damned if I know what he's on about,' said Fergus

'Never mind,' said Mairi. 'What about this weekend?'

They agreed to leave on the Friday evening, travel up river to the Dunsire forest and set up camp. The parents soon agreed and before they knew it they were waving goodbye. The journey was much the same as before, but they knew what they were doing now and reached their camping spot with ease.

Mairi who was up front yelled, 'There it is, the grassy bit, that's the beginning of the Dunsire forest.' The boat with sails down was paddled in and tied up. 'Get the sails off and unload,' shouted Fergus, 'and then get her up on the bank. That beach looking bit is easiest.'

With the tents up they felt like real explorers again. 'Pity Ann and Iain aren't here. You feel they should be,' said Pete.

'Yeah, we'll miss them,' said Mairi.

'But we have to move on,' said Fergus. 'Something to eat now and that'll be enough for today. Busy day tomorrow.'

Chapter 23 The Forest bars their Way

Next morning they were raring to go.

Breakfast finished, Fergus took them in hand. 'If this nest is here, it will be in a tree on the edge of the forest. Is that right, Pete?'

'Yes, unless there are rocky high ledges.. How it could be in a tree after 700 years is beyond me.'

'What will it look like?' said Mairi. 'The nest I mean.'

'Pete, you're the expert,' said Fergus.

'Well, it will be big - could be very big. Could be two metres high and maybe a metre and a half across. It'll be made of dead branches and sticks. Maybe green stuff woven into it.'

'Will the birds be in it?' said Scud.

'They could be and there might be eaglets. If there are, we'll leave them alone.'

'If there are,' said Fergus, 'Christiana can collect the rings on her own. This other chap, Angus Og, can help her.'

Off they went, in single file with Fergus and Mairi at either end, and Scud and Pete in the middle. It was easy as long as there was a grassy bank, but soon their way was blocked by giant hogweed, eight feet tall with big umbrella like heads and poisonous, hairy fibres up the stems.

'Watch these weeds,' said Mairi. 'They'll sting you.'

'They're like Triffids. You're sure they can't walk, are you?' said Scud.

'No, but they're dangerous.'

And when they had to go into the forest to get past them, it was mossy and wet and had crumbly, fallen tree trunks covered in orange coloured fungi that cracked and sank when they stepped on them.

All Saturday morning they worked their way into the forest, but they could not find an eagle's nest.

At mid-day they had something to eat and then set off again. They were further from the river and the forest was different now There was no giant hogweed, but snake-like shoots of bramble curled across their path. They tore their legs and gripped their clothes. Scud kept saying he hoped there were none of the plants that ate insects and things and Mairi kept telling him that was only in America or somewhere. Pete knew what he was doing though. He had a big stick and a knife and if brambles attacked him, he cut them down. But it was hard going and they were tired out by evening. The snag was that they were only half way round and still had their steps to re-trace to return to their camp.

'Can't we go through the middle of the forest?' said Scud. 'It'll be shorter.'

'Yes,' said Mairi, 'but not easy.'

'Harder than this?'

'Yes, the trees will be growing close together. It will be almost impossible to get through. Anyway, it will be dark in there.'

Off they went down the path they had beaten out during the day.

Scud kept moaning about having to walk the same route again until Fergus snapped. 'Scud, if you want to go through the forest, off you go. We'll meet you at the river.'

'Great,' said Scud and dived into the trees.

He had to struggle. The branches were whippy and kept lashing back to thrash his arms and legs. It was one branch after another and one more tree to crowd in on him and hold him back. He stopped to catch his breath and wipe away the sweat, then he gulped and went stone cold. There was a thing waving at him through the branches. It wasn't the monster was it, he thought? Never – what an idiot. That lot must have raced round and were waving at him from the other side.

He darted forward as best he could, shouting and waving, 'I see you, I see you' when a cold fear gripped his body. It was not one wave, it was not three, it was dozens waving and leaning towards him. He could not move. There were white arms, red arms, all colours. He saw long straggly ones coming straight for him, thick tough ones waiting to thump him and he could hear a whooshing, almost moaning noise that made his skin go tight. Something cracked and he was off, running and scrambling as best he could and yelling. Bleeding, banged and sprawling continually he met the others running towards him.

'What's up,' said Mairi as she grabbed him and tried to calm him down.

'It's a mon. . . monster. It's got hundreds of arms. It tried to grab me. I think it followed me.'

The three looked up quickly. There was nothing in sight.

'Are you sure it moves fast?' said Fergus. 'There's nothing here yet. Still let's get out of here.'

'Fergus, it can't move that fast if it isn't here by now,' said Mairi. 'If we're going to search this forest we better find out what we are up against.'

'Okay, but this better be true, Scud.'

They walked slowly along Scud's path into the wood. Mairi took Scud's hand, a thing he had not allowed her to do for a long time. Fergus led, armed with Pete's big stick and they cautiously advanced into the forest.

'I can't see anything,' said Fergus. 'It's windier than I expected. It's usually quite still in a forest.'

'The foresters might have cut a road in here somewhere. That might be funnelling it,' said Mairi.

'Wait a minute, what's that. Look, something white and that smell - ugh, it stinks,' said Fergus.

'It'll be blood,' said Scud.

'It's more like unwashed bodies,' said Mairi.

'Stay here, Scud,' said Fergus. 'Keep him with you, Pete.'

Fergus and Mairi, down on all fours, closing in to check it out, quietly, hardly breathing, crawled forward.

'I see it,' mouthed Fergus just when Mairi let out a peal of laughter.

'It's a Clootie Tree.'

<u>Chapter 24</u> – 'A Clootie Tree?'

'A Clootie Tree! What's a Clootie Tree?' said Fergus.

'From long ago,' said Mairi. 'They're supposed to prevent you becoming ill, I think. You tie a rag to a branch – that's what's waving.'

Scud and Pete had come up when they heard Mairi's laugh.

'What is it?' asked Scud still whispering.

'Well it's not a monster and it can't chase you,' said Mairi.

'It's weird,' said Pete.

'But some of these rags are new,' said Fergus. 'Do people still come in and tie them on?'

'They must,' said Mairi.

'Anyway, it won't harm us so we can carry on with our search,' said Mairi. 'And it doesn't move. It was the wind blowing the branches so let's get on. I'm starving.'

They walked back to camp, had a good feed and then blethered about the search.

'Do you think it's in this forest, Mairi?' said Fergus.

'I don't know. It's old enough, but there are no real clues, are there?'

'It's no' here,' said Scud. 'Christiana would be here if we were near it.'

'She doesn't know where it is. That's why we're here,' said Fergus. 'If all these people have been tramping in and out of here for hundreds of years to tie rags on that tree, it's the last place eagles would nest.'

'We'll go right round tomorrow seeing we're here,' said Mairi.

'Okay. If we don't find anything, we'll go home and try somewhere else.'

They tried next day but they did not find a nest.

'Right, that's it. Get the boat ready and then we're off,' said Fergus.

'Pity,' said Scud. 'Christiana didn't come.'

'It's about time. She should be helping,' said Fergus.

'It's not so easy to get through and she's been busy,' said Scud.

'Get through what,' said Fergus 'and we're all busy.'

'Get through from where she is. I don't know! Something happened to her. There were boats fighting, you know that.'

'What kind of boats?' said Pete.

'Galleys - sailing galleys. They are all sizes but Christiana has a Dragon boat.'

'A Dragon boat?' said Pete. 'What's that?'

'It's a chieftain's boat and it is always the biggest with the most oars. Her one has sixty-four. It's called a Dragon boat because of its size and because it has a tall dragon's head on its prow.'

They got home very quickly without a lot of time to talk and the next night they discussed things in Fergus' bedroom.

'What's next then?' he said. 'Any word from Christiana?'

'Nope, not yet,' said Scud.

'I think the Tarnlosh forest is the best bet,' said Mairi. 'It's old and it has rocky cliffs. It's big but the map will show us how to get to them. This tree business doesn't make sense to me either, Pete.'

'Yeah, it's nonsense. It's got to be cliffs'

'Need more than a weekend. It's a long way' said Fergus.

'Christiana might take us over in her Dragon boat,' said Scud.

'Aw, Scud, this is getting past it,' said Fergus. 'That's magic.'

'Well,' said Scud.

'Are we up to sailing there?' said Mairi.

'I hope so, but it is through the Pillars of Cuch,' said Fergus

'It's a summer holiday job then,' said Mairi.

'Yeah and a lot of preparation beforehand as well,' said Fergus.

'You're sure we can do it ourselves.'

'No, I'm not. I'll ask around.'

‘Christiana could come in our boat,’ said Scud. ‘She’ll know how to sail there,’

‘I bet she does,’ said Fergus ‘but where is she?’

Chapter 25 The Dragon Boat

'Hello Scud, no luck?'

He was walking up the side of the bay, a bit fed up because things were not going well. Last weekend had not been a success and he felt a bit of a fool over the monster – everyone was pulling his leg about it – and there had been no sign of Christiana.

He had just sat down for a rest when there she was right in front of him.

'Hi! – where have you been?'

'These brothers of mine. They still will not accept me as Chief. They tried to kidnap me. They will think twice before they try that again.'

'It's important, isn't it – the Double Helix and all that.'

'It means I am who I say I am. I will never be accepted as Queen without it.'

'Well, we couldn't find the eagles' nest. Not at Dunsire anyway. And Mairi and Pete think it can't be in a tree. Pete thinks it will be on a cliff ledge and if there are trees involved, the cliff will be in a forest. What do you think?'

'Makes sense. That stone pillar outside your village might give you a clue.'

'I'll check it but we are thinking of going to Tarnlosh. The snag is that it is through the Pillars of Cush. Fergus is trying to find out about them.'

'I could take you in my boat and show you the way.'

'Could you. That would be great. Fergus thought you couldn't do that.'

'I could do it for you, you understand. I am pretty sure I could not do it for them.'

'I've missed you, Christiana. I thought you weren't coming back.'

'No Scud. I will never leave now. I wish you could be King when I prove I am Christiana of the Isles. You would be Scud of the Isles, but I better go now. I've got to keep an eye on these brothers of mine. I will be in touch to take you through the Pillars.'

Scud felt great. He was beginning to like Christiana an awful lot. 'Scud of the Isles,' he thought – 'that was something.'

* * *

'Let us go, Scud. My boat is at the pier.' It was Christiana in front of him again.

'Are you back already?'

.'Come on, I will show you how to go through the Pillars.'

Scud climbed aboard the Dragon Boat with a very regal Christiana. She was very Queen-like and in command. She was dressed like her crew in a saffron kilt, linen shirt and calfskin jerkin, belt and dirk, but a golden tiara and a fur trimmed purple open robe made her stand out from those around her.

'Welcome to my craft, Lord Scud for within my Kingdom you are declared a Lord and must take your place at my right hand upon this sailing platform.'

She signalled to the sailing master and the boat was neatly backed into the stream to catch the wind. The towering, rectangular sail was hoisted and the boat was on its way.

'This voyage is easy,' said Christiana. 'You just have to solve the problem of getting through the Pillars.'.

'What is the Cuch anyway?' said Scud.

'No man or woman knows, but they left behind a legacy so fearsome that sailors dread to breach their door. With the tide – the normal way to go through a gap like this - the door is locked. To make it on the ebb you must have the key. But unless you stand firm when first you sight the dreaded portals you will never resist their challenge They stand aloof and tall on either side and dare any boat to breech their right.'

'You must like it when the sail pulls like this,' said Scud.

'Normally we give the rowers a rest when we use the sail but we must catch the ebb tide.'

'Will we have oars when we go through,' said Scud. 'Will it be all right?'

'Do not worry. If you do it right it is easy. The Cuch had to get in and out. It is like having the right key for a lock but make sure you have a strong wind before you attempt it.'

In no time at all they neared the other coast. 'It is coming up now, Scud,' said Christiana as she pointed it out just to the left of the Dragon's head. Slowly the Pillars came in view increasing in size to the fearsome sight they were.

The Pillars were huge – one on each side of the entrance – and tall and slim. The rock was grey and shiny with long ridges running down the sides.

At their base they were attached to the mainland rocks themselves huge and massive; green and grey, purple and yellow and here and there blotched with red – an intimidating sight.

The water surged and swung, tortured and twisted as it forced its way between the sentinel towers.

'Hell's Bells,' said Scud. 'Not through there!'

Chapter 26 The Key

'It is easy,' said Christiana.

'Easy!' said Scud, 'Look at it.'

'Just watch and you will see. Use the key and you will glide through. A strong underwater current from the north side is meeting the water rushing out and creating a back eddy going right up the far side and going in. If you have the courage to steer right through this to the other side you will find it.'

'If you say so,' said a worried Scud.

'Watch. We will use nothing but the sails.'

'Here we go. Right up the middle until the mast and the right hand pillar are in line. Wait; wait; keep your eye on the mast. Wait.'

The boat started to bucket about. The bow jumped from side to side and water slewed on board.

'It's getting dangerous,' said Scud looking at the water all around them and ahead.

'This is as bad as it gets,' said Christiana. 'Get your eye right up to the mast and as soon as it is in line with the Pillar, shout.'

With one eye on the water and the other peering from the mast to the shore and two hands clinging to what ever was handy, Scud anxiously kept watch. It was wet where he stood and slippery and the water was still coming aboard in sheets.

Suddenly, he shouted 'Now' as the mast and the Pillar lined up.

Christiana pushed the tiller away from her and put the boat into the shore; there the water was slack, but moving slowly in through the gap.

'This is something' said Scud. 'I can't believe it, but we are going in and there's the forest.'

'It is a very narrow band, hardly noticeable, and it does not last long,' said Christiana, 'but remember to do it on the ebb.'

The Forest of Tarnlosh started on the opposite shore and stretched for miles.

'It's big,' said Scud. 'We'll have a job finding the cliffs, but Mairi and Pete are getting a map of it with the cliffs marked on it. Here, wait a minute. How do we get out of here?'

'There is no problem; just reverse everything.'

They sailed over to the far shore to give Scud a better sight of the forest and sailed homewhen the tide turned.

'Thanks Christiana. I'll tell Fergus and we'll get things going.' He stepped off the boat and waved as the Dragon boat sailed.

* * *

'What are you doing here?' said Fergus as he came on Scud lying at the side of the bay.

'I was thinking about Christiana.'

'I bet you were.'

'Here Fergus, I know how to get to Tarnosh through the Pillars. Christiana took me.'

'You were on her boat?'

'Yes, she took me through the Pillars. It's easy. I've got the key.'

'Well, that's as maybe but I've been asking around and it's supposed to be very difficult - too much for us.'

'Not with the key. It's easy.'

Scud told Fergus how to do it and then again when they were with Mairi and Pete.

'Scud,' said Fergus. 'I don't know what to believe. What do you think, Mairi?'

I'm sure Scud is not telling lies. It's too dangerous but I must admit I would like some proof. It's supposed to be a terrible place – the Pillars. You could get drowned.'

'I'm telling you. I've been through. Christiana says that the worst thing is the fear, the terrible sight of it. You've got to trust the key.'

'What about you, Pete?' said Fergus. 'Are you willing to try?'

‘I don’t know. What do you think, Mairi? Where can you get proof?’

‘Well, in a book or something,’ said Mairi.

‘What about the pillar outside the village?’ said Pete. ‘You said that was how they wrote things down years ago.’

In a flash, Mairi turned to Fergus, ‘That’s it,’ she said.

Chapter 27 The Pillars

They checked. Thoroughly.

Right at the foot of the monument, he found the pictures that told it all.

The stone was covered with little figures. Men with raised spears and shields were battles; ships with bulging sails meant journeys; and kings and queens were represented by their crowns.

'Look!' shouted Scud. 'Can you see, underneath the crown, two rings stuck together - a double helix?'

They all went quiet and stared at each other.

'That's something,' said Fergus. 'There's been a message all the time.'

'Not a message,' said Mairi, 'a statement. It's saying that to have the crown you must have the double helix as well.'

'I can't see any mention of eagles,' said Fergus.

'You won't ,' said Mairi. 'The statue was built long before Dougal gave the rings to the Abbey.'

'There they are,' said Scud. He didn't shout or raise his voice. He just said quietly, 'The Pillars', knowing that it showed that his story was true.

'Can't see anything about the key, though,' said Fergus.

Mairi rubbed the stone clear and poked out little bits of grey lichen. 'Look at these lines.'

'That's it,' said Scud. 'The key. See the lines coming out through the Pillars. It's the ebb tide and these other lines hitting it and turning right up the side. See, they fade out when they get through the Pillar. That's the eddy.'

'Looks good, Fergus,' said Mairi. 'Do you see it?'

Yeah, I see what you mean. He might be right.'

That night they gathered in Fergus' bedroom and worked out what they were going to do.

'I'm convinced,' said Fergus. 'What about you, Mairi?'

'I said I wanted to read something about it and I have.'

'Pete?'

'Yeah, seems right.'

'Okay, Scud. We'll do it. Nobody will believe us though. Better keep it quiet. No adults.'

Arrangements were made and they set off as soon as the school holidays started. The parents saw them off. They knew that they were going over the Firth on a camping trip but nothing else. The coastguard was notified and they took a radio with them. The Pillars were never mentioned.

Fergus kept on course right across the Firth and with the wind in their favour they made good time.

'It's not far now,' said Scud. 'It's a terrible sight, but don't worry it's easy with the key.' When they first saw it, Mairi and Pete were shocked into silence. Fergus did not say much either. Sailing things did not usually bother him, but when he saw the water between the Pillars, he quietly said to Scud, 'we can't sail through that – the tide's against us.'

'We can. Trust me. Sail for the middle point between the Pillars and when I shout, turn hard to starboard. 'It said a lot for them that they did just that, but they were very scared. The ebb was piling up against the wind, there was white water everywhere and the boat was bucketing all over the place.

The change after the turn mystified them when suddenly the water was flat and running in a different direction.

'What about that!' said Mairi.

'It's no' real,' said Fergus, 'and on the ebb too. Scud, I was wrong. There's something in all this,'

Pete still kept quiet.

'There's the forest,' said Scud. 'Where are we going to land?'

'The map shows two cliffs in the forest on the west side,' said Mairi, 'and a beach along here a bit.'

'That'll do,' said Fergus. 'We're going west now.'

They sailed down the coast for about a mile, identified the beach and landed. The boat was pulled up, everyone stretched their legs and shook themselves. They were exhausted.

'Mairi, do you fancy something to eat first. I'll cook it if you give me the stuff.'

‘It’s alright, Fergus. Pitch the tents and make a fireplace. We’ll have a cup of tea before I make something.’

It has to be said: it took them a while to calm down. The passage had not been easy and it stretched their willpower to make it. Eventually round the fire and with Mairi’s bacon and eggs and a lot of resilience they recovered.

‘Spread out the map, Mairi and show us where these cliffs are,’ said Fergus.

‘Are we not going to look at trees then?’ said Scud.

‘We’ll go up the side of the forest and check for a nest,’ said Mairi, ‘and mark off what we’ve done. When we are opposite the cliffs we’ll go inland. We’ll check all the cliffs first and only do the forest edges on the way to them. If we don’t find the nest on the cliffs, we’ll finish the edges. Okay.’

‘Christiana included, I hope.’ said Fergus. ‘Where is she anyway? She’s the reason for all this.’

They all agreed or they were too tired to argue.

‘Are there any Clootie trees in this forest?’ said Scud.

‘Never mind, Scud, they can’t chase you,’ said Fergus.

‘Still, it will be wise to be ready for anything’ said Mairi.

Chapter 28 This is Dangerous

'You sure about this?' said Scud.

'I don't know.' said Mairi.' It's just that the forest is very old. It goes right back to before Christiana's time.'

They worked their way right up the side of Tarnlosh in single file all looking for a big nest. Fergus led the way with his compass in his hand. Scud was next wishing that Christiana was by his side. Pete followed him well prepared for trouble with his big stick and Mairi brought up the rear.

They must have walked about 3000 metres when Mairi shouted, 'the turn is about here. Check it, Fergus.' He had taken a bearing the night before and knew what his compass should read when they were opposite the cliffs.

'This is it,' he said and turned into the forest.

Going through the forest was harder. Sometimes it was clear but usually trees and more often springy branches held them back. Still they had done this before and just got on with it.

It was hard work, but eventually Mairi shouted, 'nearly there,' when the forest started to open up to reveal the cliff. Actually it was a hill with a cliff on one side.

'We're there,' said Mairi. 'Looks promising.'

'It's steep but there's a ledge off to the right,' said Fergus

'I think there are more ledges,' said Pete. 'See round to the right of the first one.'

'I don't see a nest,' said Scud.

'Nope,' said Mairi, 'but we better go up and look.'

The first two ledges were fairly easy climbs but the top one was difficult.

'I think we'll have to go to the top and lower someone down,' said Fergus.

They had a rope with them but who was going down the rock face.

'The lightest should go down,' said Fergus. 'I better stay at the top to help hold the rope.'

'No, that's Scud,' said Pete. 'I'll go. I'm not much heavier.'

They agreed and started to lower Pete down the cliff with a bowline under his arms. He slid over the edge; face inward and swinging slightly from side to side.

'Slowly,' he shouted. 'I don't know if I fancy this. Take it easy.'

Inch by inch he was lowered down, with his feet on the cliff to keep him from being scraped on the rock, until he reached the ledge.

'It's no' here,' he called, 'bring me up.'

At the top they had a confab.

'We couldn't expect to find it first time,' said Mairi. 'Where's the next cliff?'

After a quick meal they set off on a compass bearing right into the heart of the forest – the oldest part.

It got darker and darker. The trees blocked out the light and they had to fight to get past them. Branches snapped in their faces, stung their legs and were forever trying to hold on to them. Long twisted roots tripped them up and seemed as if they wanted to grab them by the ankle. It was deathly quiet.

'There's light ahead,' shouted Fergus. 'We're nearly out.'

'But they were not. It was a small, circular clearing not much more than four metres across with no trees or bushes in it at all.

'It's like a chapel with a sky roof,' said Scud.

And it looked almost mystical with a beam of light pouring down inside its funnel of trees. They were spellbound and stood, unable for a moment to talk, bewildered and stunned by the scene.

'It's a stone circle,' whispered Mairi. 'Look at the rocks.'

There were boulders set in two circles one inside the other and covered in a green/grey almost bluish lichen.

'What are these circles for anyway?' asked Fergus.

'Don't know,' said Mairi. People aren't sure.'

'I think there were sacrifices in stone circles,' said Pete.

'They didn't kill people, did they?' said Scud.

'I don't know, I don't know,' whispered Mairi. 'Let's go.'

They left quickly and fought their way to the other cliff. When they found it they sank down gratefully in a heap.

'Didn't like that place,' said Scud.

'I'm knackered,' said Fergus. 'This better be true as well, Scud, all this stuff.'

But when they recovered and saw the ledge on the face of a kind of precipice.

'This is more like it.' said Fergus. 'Eagles might nest here. It's not called a nest, is it Pete?'

'It's called an eyrie and how we're going to get up there I don't know.'

The rock face was very steep. There were hand holds but it would be a difficult climb and they only had rope for equipment.

'Well, we can't climb it today,' said Mairi, 'and I don't fancy trekking back to camp. Wish we had brought sleeping bags.'

'What have we got?' said Pete. 'Food, water?' We'll need those.'

'Well, there's a tin of meat and some bread in the rucksack and crisps and a bottle of orange. That'll do. Where are we going to sleep though?'

'I can make beds out of that bracken,' said Pete, 'It'll be fine to lie on. We've no bags or blankets, but if we wear all the clothes we've got and pile on more bracken, we'll be fine.'

And that is what they did. They had to do it in a hurry because darkness came down quickly in the forest. They slept closely together for heat. It wasn't exactly warm – Scud even had his woollen sailing cap on – but they didn't notice. They were all together.

It was just as well because it wasn't the cold that got to them, it was the forest. It was a scary place.

Chapter 29 The Forest Moves

The forest moved all night.

The undergrowth rustled: small animals scurried on the prowl; the tops of the trees waved and danced; and there was an owl about.

'I don't know about bloomin' eagles,' said Fergus, 'but if that owl hoots again it'll get my boot where it doesn't want it.'

They were stiff and sore in the morning, wishing they had gone back to camp.

'But we're here now,' said Mairi. 'We can start to climb right after breakfast.'

'Yeah, the climb,' said Fergus. 'How are we going to get up there?'

'I know,' said Scud.

'You would,' said Fergus. 'Has she been here again?'

'I don't know how I know but I do. Maybe she didn't want to wake me.'

'Okay. How is it to be done?'

'Well there are two ledges, one we can't see from here. It's very small and if I can reach it I can get across to the one we can see. There's a crack in the rock leading to the first ledge and a small person could get up it and that's me.'

'We'll see. Let's find it first,' said Mairi.

They soon spotted it and there was just enough space for Scud to get his back on one side and his feet on the other to inch his way upwards.

'Can you do it, Scud?' said Fergus. 'Mind you, it's not a lot of good if you can't get across to the other ledge.'

'I'll do it.'

'If there is a nest,' said Mairi, 'lower the rope and we'll come up and help.'

Scud tied his boots on tightly – their rubber soles were essential for grip – and he borrowed Pete's jacket to protect his back. He got into the crack and jammed himself in with his feet on one side and his back on the other. He pushed against his feet and forced his back up and then against his back to force his feet up. It was not easy. His legs ached and his back was rubbed sore but he made it.

'I'm there,' he shouted. 'It's very small.'

'Rest for a minute,' said Mairi. 'Can you get across?'

'Yes, when I get my breath back. It'll be easy.'

'I can see right along it,' and his voice cracked as he shouted, 'there's a nest.'

That was the end of the rest. He edged along and went over to the bigger ledge.

'Careful, Scud,' shouted Mairi. 'Don't go if there are eaglets.'

'No, it's empty. Can't see any rings either,' he shouted as he peered into the nest.'

'Lower the rope,' said Fergus. 'The rings will be mixed up with the sticks and stuff.'

Scud got a bowline loop round a rock and all three came up, but they could not see the rings either.

'Wait a minute,' said Mairi. 'How do we know if this is the right one.'

'If the rings are mixed up in this lot, it's the right one,' said Fergus, 'and if they're no', we look for another one.'

'If they're no here,' said Pete, 'we've got to find gold marked eagles.'

'Not on your life,' said Fergus. 'No standing on this ledge anyway.'

And then Scud found them – feathers, brown with gold marks. When he laid them alongside each other they formed a gold line.

'I never know how you do that,' said Fergus. 'There is a bit of the magician in you.'

'Fergus, never mind all that. This is it,' said Mairi 'and the eagles have gone. I wonder how long they stay on a nest. 'We better get started searching. Remember the Helix is very small.'

'And don't destroy the nest,' said Pete. 'The eagles will need it again.'

They lifted the sticks, examined each layer and probed the difficult bits.

'It must be here,' said Mairi. 'This is an eagles' nest and the eagles have gold rings round their legs. That's what we want Scud, isn't it.'

'It'll be here.'

They searched again right down to the rock the nest was sitting on.

'Did you see any ledges on the other side, Scud?' said Pete.

'Nope. This is it.'

They searched right along the ledge, Nothing. They started on the nest again but it defeated them.

'It's no' here,' said Fergus.

'It was' said Scud.

'Well, it's not now.'

'It must have been moved.

'Moved! Who by?'

'I don't know. I'll ask Christiana.'

'Yeah. No, don't tell me. She's coming, is she?'

'There's no need to fall out,' said Mairi. 'There's an explanation somewhere. I think somebody's been here before us.'

'Scud, how do you get in touch with Christiana?'

'I don't know. She just appears.'

'There must be some way to send her a message.'

'I'll think about it.'

'Right everybody,' said Mairi. 'We can't do any more here. We'll share out what's left of the food and head back to the camp.'

They were disappointed and did not know what to do, but Mairi said, 'We're going back to camp. We don't need to go home. Scud might get through to Christiana and we'see what she says."

It was back along the same way, the same difficult route. They came to the circle again and it looked as mysterious as ever. The sun was shining and there was a beam of light coming down the funnel of the trees. It lit up the circle and showed up the damp condensation rising from the plants and moss drying in the sun. It struck clouds of insects almost like a searchlight picking out aeroplanes at night. They were still uneasy about it and hurried past. Then, when they were about 100 metres beyond it, Scud stopped and shouted, 'I'm going back for a minute. I'll catch you up.'

He did not know why but the circle excited him now. At the circle he sat on one of the walls and there she was - Christiana.

Chapter 30 Where are the Rings?

'Thank goodness. I need you,' said Scud.

'What's up? You look terrible,' said Christiana.

'We've found the nest. The eagles have gold circles on their feathers, but there are no rings.'

'No!' said Christiana. 'What happened? You searched the nest?'

'Three times. There's nothing there. You look different.'

Christiana glowed. Light surrounded her like a big wheel. 'It is just the journey through the circle,' she said. 'It is easier to get through if there is a circle but small ones are harder than big ones. There is another, bigger one nearby and it might be easier. They are very ancient places – a lot older than me – and very powerful. But never mind all that. What about the Double Helix?'

'Mairi thinks someone has moved it. What do you think we should do now?'

'Somebody moved it. I never thought of that. Mairi might be right.'

'Who would know?'

'Took me long enough to find out about the eagles. It had to be someone who knew about them and who had a powerful need to own the Double Helix – just like me.'

'Can I just get this right. We're looking for two rings stuck together in the shape of a double helix.'

'Yes.'

'Well I don't know,' said Scud. 'There was nothing like that in the nest.'

'I've got it' said Christiana, 'Jane, my Aunt, had the same trouble I'm having. She was supposed to be chief – she didn't have brothers – but her Uncle just took over and she left to get married. I never met her. Maybe she hid them to stop him getting them.'

'Where would she put them?'

'I do not know. I'll have to think about it. Look, go back to your camp and I'll reach you there.'

'I'll have to tell the others.'

'That is all right, but do not mention that stone circles can be a way to contact me. It can be dangerous if other people try to use them.'

They parted and Scud ran after Fergus, Mairi and Pete.

'I've spoken to Christiana,' Scud said when he caught up. 'She's thought of something and is away to check. She'll be in touch.'

Fine,' said Fergus. 'We need a rest anyway. Let's get back to camp.'

'Was she surprised?' said Mairi.

'Yes. It's something to do with her Aunt,' said Scud.

When they arrived at their camp they checked everything, made sure the boat was okay, had a quick feed and flopped.

Next morning was a beautiful, sunny morning. The creepy forest, the hard bracken beds and the mysterious circle seemed far away.

' I'm going fishing,' said Fergus. 'Anybody coming?'

'I'll have to be here in case Christiana turns up,' said Scud.

'I'll stay with him,' said Mairi. 'You go, Pete. If you catch anything, we'll have it tonight.'

Scud tided up and Mairi made a cup of tea and then sat down and talked about the whole thing.

'You're really sold on this, aren't you, Scud?'

'Yep, I think I am. It's Christiana, we really get on. I'm not sure what we can do about it and I don't understand it all yet.'

'It's difficult,' said Mairi. 'I mean if she was a girl in your class at school it would be easy. She would be your girl friend. You could sail with her instead of me.'

'I like sailing with you, Mairi. I think we'll be good.'

'I know. We've got the Regatta when we get back but this is different. She's your girl friend and she's a good sailor, but I don't see how you could go in for the Regatta together.'

'No, that's the problem,' said a worried Scud. 'There's no' a lot around here we can do together. And I'm no' sure she'd want that. She's Christiana of the Isles and she wants me to go back with her and be Scud of the Isles – a Prince.'

Mairi did not know what to say - it was getting a bit deep.

'I don't know how that would work out. It seems as difficult as going in for the Regatta together.'

'Did she tell you when she would be coming back? We can't stay here for ever. We've only got about three days food.'

'No,' said Scud. 'We'll see what happens.'

They had a lazy time recovering from their exertions and Fergus and Pete turned up in the afternoon with two big sea trout.

'Any news?' said Fergus.

'No,' said Mairi, 'not yet, but the fish look good. They'll help out our stores. In fact, you might have to eat fish every day if we stay here for a while.'

An evening meal of sea trout and potatoes was voted smashing and they went to bed happy, full-up and contented.

Next morning, Scud sat up hurriedly and shouted, 'she's been!'

They were all getting accustomed to these announcements now and gathered round for the news.

'It was her Aunt Jane. Well it might have been her great aunt.'

'Never mind all that,' said Fergus. 'What about the rings?'

'Okay. Her Great Aunt Jane had the same trouble as she had trying to claim the Chieftainship. She set out to find the rings for the same reason but never produced them. Christiana's grandfather's brother, Ruiri was too strong for her.'

'This is getting a bit much,' said Fergus. 'I've never heard of so many grandfathers, cousins and aunts.' How many of them are there?'

'Quiet, Fergus.' said Mairi. 'We're getting somewhere. Go on, Scud.'

'Well, her Aunt Jane left and got married and Christiana thinks she may have hidden the rings to stop Ruiri getting them. She says Jane wouldn't have brought them home in case Ruiri got them. The possession of the Double Helix would really have made him King.'

'Christiana's not absolutely sure but she thinks they will be buried near the nest and the story is that they are at a spot where the sun strikes at twelve.'

'Oh! That's great,' said Fergus. 'The sun strikes everywhere at twelve o'clock.'

'I know, Fergus,' said Mairi, 'but it must be somewhere special. Somewhere that gets the sun only at twelve o'clock. That's a good clue. Is Christiana going to help?'

'She's coming back if she finds out more.'

'Right,' said Mairi. 'First light tomorrow, it's back to the nest.'

Chapter 31 The Sun Strikes

The path was now well worn.

They made their way into the forest up their old route and soon were standing at the bottom of the cliff.

'There's no point going up there again,' said Mairi. 'There must be somewhere else that made a good hiding place. The sun's the clue.'

'What about a cave?' said Pete. 'The sun won't get in a cave very often.'

'A list. We need a list of likely places,' said Mairi.

Scud wanted to say the Stone Circle in the wood, but Christiana had said not to talk about it. But wait a minute, he thought, there is another stone circle – a big one.

'There's another stone circle near here,' he said. 'We could look there.'

'How do you know,' said Fergus.

Christiana said so.'

'You're no telling us everything, are you?'

'I am. She just mentioned there was a bigger one near here.'

'Right,' said Mairi, 'that's another place. Anywhere else?'

'What's this on the map?' said Pete – 'looks like a well or water or something.'

'Well it won't be a swimming pool out here. Where's the bit that tells you what the symbols mean?' said Fergus.

'There it is,' said Pete. 'It's a watery place. That's sounds a possible; people used to throw valuable things in watery places as gifts to their gods, - you know, sacred places.'

'Sacred,' said Fergus. 'It'll no' be that. It'll no' be in the middle of a forest in stinking water. And how would you find a helix again in a place like that. They found the pools, but they did not look like places to hide rings. The sun's no' likely to strike here at twelve. It's not going to strike in here at all. It'll no' be here.'

'Yeah,' said Mairi. 'Jane wouldn't put it here if she wanted it back. You're right.'

Luckily the other stone circle was marked on the map as an ancient monument.

'On the way look out for caves,' said Mairi, and using the compass they found the new circle quite easily. It was big - much bigger than the one they found earlier.

'This is some place,' said Scud. 'I bet it belonged to Christiana's people.'

'It might have,' said Pete, 'but it would be here long before her time.'

There were three circles set inside each other in a large open space. Some of the stones were missing and others had fallen over. The centre space had three stones, one on top of two others like a small table.

'It's certainly big,' said Mairi, 'and there's a kind of an entrance.'

On the outer circle two tall stones about two metres high had another lying on top making it look like a doorway.

'And there's a path or something going straight to the centre,' said Scud.

It was an awesome place, not complete because of the fallen and missing stones, but with an aura and prescience about it. Scud started running and scurrying all over the place, shouting and pointing at things. Certainly the more you looked, the more you saw how it had once been.

'It's great, fantastic,' he kept shouting. 'What a place!'

'Take it easy, Scud,' said Fergus.

'You'd almost think he knew the place,' said Mairi. 'He certainly seems to feel at home here.'

'What is it, Scud?' she said. 'Do you know something about this place?'

'Can you no' feel it, Mairi? It grips you. I bet you they're here.'

'You look as if you know. Did Christiana tell you?'

'No, she didn't. She just said there was another circle. She did say it was powerful.' He jerked round – 'Is she here?'

‘Just relax, Scud, for a minute. I want to think. Fergus, help him to calm down.’

‘Help him! He’s away wi’ the fairies.’

‘No, he’s not. He’s away somewhere though. Still this is a likely place. But food first and then a search.’

They sprawled on the grass near the entrance and took in the scene. It was a glorious day. The sun was shining, on the trees, on them and on the circle. ‘Settle down, Scud,’ said Mairi. ‘We’ll get it.’ Just take it easy for a bit.’

But Scud could not take his mind off things and kept looking at the circle as if he expected something to happen. He could see it all from where he sat. The side nearest him was in the shade but as the sun moved round towards midday it lit up more and more of the outer circle.

He was watching it when suddenly the rays hit the entrance and shot up the path into the little stone table at the centre. The stones were illuminated brilliantly.

‘Mairi,’ he said. ‘What time is it?’

‘It’s twelve o’clock.’

‘I know where the Golden Helix is.’

Chapter 32 The Find.

Scud did not move.

He just said it again. 'I know where it is.'

'Where?' shouted Fergus.

'In the centre underneath the stool thing. Look, the sun's gone right in it and it's twelve o'clock.'

They all stared. Fergus leapt for the path, but was stopped by Scud.

'Don't touch it, Ferrie. DON'T!' he said in a voice that did not even sound like Scud. 'Leave it. We need help.'

Fergus stopped and looked round more at the voice than the person. 'Okay' was all he said,

'What do you want us to do?' said Mairi.

'Wait for Christiana. I'll try and get her. It's dangerous.'

Mairi nodded and Scud set out for the little circle.

She was there. 'You have found it, haven't you? I came as soon as I knew. Did you touch it?'

'No. Why?'

'Anybody touching it would have been returned to the 14th century with me. I wish you had.'

'I thought that. I don't think I can, Christiana. I'd like to but I can't.'

'I know, Scud. Forgive me. It is very difficult and it is not often done. Never mind, I'll come and take the Double Helix away. Thank everyone for me and tell them I will be taking up my throne. I'll definitely be Christiana, the Lady of Garmoran from now on. Goodbye, Scud.'

A dejected Scud walked back to the others.

'Where have you been?' said Fergus. 'You've been ages.'

'No, I haven't. Anyway, it's all fixed.'

'You've seen her then,' said Mairi.

'Yes.' She's going to take it away and claim her throne officially. She's maybe even been.'

'What!' shouted Fergus. 'Are you saying she's taken them away while we've been standing here?'

Fergus started to run to the centre of the circle. There was nothing there except brown earth that looked fresh – but no Helix.

'I don't believe it,' said Fergus. 'I do not believe any of it. Are you telling me that we have come all this way for nothing?'

'No, Fergus, we found them but they're not ours. Christiana's taken them.'

'She might at least have let us look at them.'

'No, it was too dangerous. If you had touched them you would instantly have gone back to the 14th century. Still you'd probably have ended up as a famous sea warrior.'

'What!'

'I told you it was dangerous. Anyway Christiana says thank you for all we've done.'

'Of course,' said Mairi, 'we said finding the Double Helix would be the proof of it all and we haven't seen it. But I believe it. I don't know how it all happens but I do believe it.'

'Me too,' said Pete.

'Well, I know something unbelievable is going on,' said Fergus, 'but what it is I don't know. It's no' real.'

'What now then, Scud?' said Mairi. 'Back home?'

'Yes.' I don't know when I'll see Christiana again. She wanted me to go back with her but I couldn't. I don't think I'll ever see her again.'

Back they went out through the Pillars and across the Firth.

'Good trip?' said Mum when they got home. 'I had a bad dream about you the other night. I got scared but something kept saying, "They're fine, they're fine". It was like a non-stop train. Anyway, you are here.'

'What I couldn't understand,' said Dad, 'was that we both had the same dream on the same night. You were sailing into a gap and the water looked impossible – looked familiar though. But you made it. Got a good night's sleep after that.'

The four of them sat that night in Fergus' bedroom.

'What do we do now?' said Mairi.

'Well,' said Fergus, 'something is happening. That's definite. I don't understand how, but I know what to do now. It's Scud's baby. He handles it and we all go racing as soon as possible. It's the Regatta in a fortnight. Five races, one a day. Same crews?'

'Yes,' said Scud. 'I want to see Christiana again, but I want to win the Regatta. I'm in.'

'Pete?'

'Yeah, that's it. You and me again, Fergus?'

'Mairi. Are you crewing for Scud?'

'Oh yes.'

'Right, that's it,' said Fergus. 'It's time we got into it. We've been away for days. Tomorrow. First thing. What's the tide like?'

High water's around half past twelve,' said Mairi.

'Nine o'clock then. Dinghy Park. General sail to get the cobwebs off; then round the buoys practise; and a race between us for speed tuning.'

And that is how things were settled - or so they thought.

Chapter 33 The Absent Spirit

They threw themselves into it.

They were not rusty, but they had to gear up. This was now and they had their own battles to fight. There would be sailors from all over the country but in the small boat class they had a chance.

Fergus was a front runner. Scud was an unknown. He was good: athletic and graceful he moved like a gymnast. But, and it was a big but, he was young. He was still learning and he still made mistakes.

All that fortnight they trained and sailed from morn till night and, by the day of the Regatta, they were as ready as they could be.

There were 78 boats entered but, of course, not all of them were in the small boat class. The club was full of sailors and they all looked like champions. It was a bit overpowering.

'They all seem to be good,' said Scud.

'Nah,' said Fergus. 'Don't let them get to you and don't get excited. Keep to yourselves. Go and see to your boat. If anybody tries anything, tell them they're rubbish.'

But Scud was nervous. He had been in big things before but only as a crew for Fergus. Now he was a skipper.

The practice race was first. They knew it was the place to make your mistakes before the races counted, but not as many as Scud made. Mairi tried to help but he went from one disaster to another.

First of all, in the first race, as he was coming up to the start he was sure he was too early. He went about and was left pointing the wrong way when the gun fired.

He was 22nd out of 26 at the first buoy. Mistake after mistake followed and he was 2nd last at the finish.

Fergus and Pete were third and came ashore well pleased with themselves.

'I hope you got that out of your system, Scud,' said Fergus. 'You sailed a right one there.'

'He wasn't so bad,' said Mairi. 'It was tough out there.'

'He was rubbish,' said Fergus.

When the first counting race started Scud was even more nervous. He manoeuvred carefully, kept out of trouble and got off in the second line, 10th.

The first leg was a true beat and Fergus sailed it beautifully to round the first mark in second place and kept that position throughout.

There was no doubt about it, Scud wasn't himself at all. He sailed like a robot, correctly but slow. His go-a-bouts had no zip. Coming into the fourth mark, he made no challenge for "water" and the outside boat forced him on to the buoy. He had to round it again as a penalty. He was lifeless – you would think he was drugged. Mairi could do nothing with him and he finished up fifteenth.

'What's wrong with you!' shouted Fergus when they came in. 'Mairi, waken him up.'

They tied up and trudged wearily along to the club to sign off. When she got him in a corner, she tried again.

'What is it, Scud? What's wrong? Is it me? You've got no life in you.'

'I don't know. I'm trying. I'm not making many mistakes.'

'But you're lifeless. You're not challenging anybody. You're letting them get away with everything. It's not you.'

'I'll get it. I'll get it tomorrow. You'll see,' he said desperately.

The same thing happened. Not bad, but not good - tenth.

Fergus was first and he and Pete were congratulated all round.

'You'll need to do something, Scud,' said Mairi. 'You're missing Christiana, aren't you? Do you wish you had gone back with her?'

'No, I couldn't have. It's all a muddle. You can't go back but I miss her. She's Christiana of the Isles now and it's somebody else I know. I'll never hear from her again.'

Next morning, Mairi had Scud out early to try and rev him up. They were first out – practising runs into the line; getting their timing right; testing the wind; picking a good spot on the line.

Scud seemed all right, but would he do it when the race started.

The first gun boomed and then the five. At the one minute he was out of position again and Mairi despaired - not again she thought. He turned late, but suddenly sprang upright like a coiled spring when he heard a voice bellowing in his ear, 'Go! Get up! You are off the wind. Up – and tight.'

Scud reacted, hauled his wind and moved fast. He glanced at Mairi but she had obviously heard nothing. She felt the movement though and sensed the change. In came her jib in time with Scud and they were off.

Even Fergus felt it. He wanted the best position on the line, but lost it to the unexpected challenge from his now impudent brother.

Scud took the windward mark to lead the fleet and never looked back. He led the fleet from start to finish and if ever he felt like settling back no doubt a persistent voice in his ear kept him to his task. Who knows?

He was first – he had arrived on the scene.

'Well done, Mairi.' said Fergus. 'Kick him up the backside, did you? Do it again tomorrow. If I'm going to be beaten, it better be him.'

Actually at that stage Scud had helped Fergus. His win kept the two other leading contenders in check.

Scud was a new man. Everything he did showed life and energy and his boat moved like a thing possessed.

'What a change,' said Mairi. 'It's not me. Something's happened. I don't get it, but never mind. Tomorrow, here we come.'

And they did. You never saw the like. He took them at the start, at the marks and on the beat. The other boats attacked relentlessly, but time after time he outmanoeuvred them. He always knew what was going to happen next.

He planed the boat on the top of the waves till it almost flew. He took the right course on every beat and on the runs with his spinnaker flying he flew like a giant bird.

They hailed him at the end. The pier was lined with spectators and they cheered him until he was safely in the dinghy park.

It wasn't enough though. Fergus and Pete won the series but it raised Scud and Mairi to the runner-up position. At the prize giving, when they went up for their cups, Fergus jumped up and raised their arms in triumph.

After it was all over Mairi whispered to Scud, 'I've got it. Christiana was in the boat as well. 'You haven't lost her after all, have you?'

THE CALL OF THE HELIX

PART FOUR

THE CIRCLE OF CUCH

Lord Scud, my friend and sometime master,
I return to you.
Our history is hidden in our bones,
Our genes speak out.
My kingdom is in peril from the sea,
I need your help.

Christiana,
14th Cent. Sailor and
Lady of Garmoran

Chapter 34 He bends to the wind.

Scud bent low into the wind.

He could hardly stand as the wind blew and gusted on to the pier at the side of the club. It buffeted the houses and tore at the boats lying to their moorings in the bay. The tide was coming in with the wind and the boats had swung to face the parallel forces.

'They'll be in trouble, Fergus, when the tide turns.'

After their great achievements at the Regatta the Ospreys were paying a little back to the club by doing rescue duty with the club coxswain.

'And why not,' Mr. Stodart used to say to a worried Mrs. Stodart. 'They're good sailors. Let them be.'

'I know, Dad, but they're young to be going out in some of the weather the rescue boat goes out in.'

'Young! Weather! Have you seen what they go out in? I saw Mairi sailing with Pete. She might look like a princess, but she was throwing that boat about like a pea in a jar.'

'I wish she would tie up her hair though,' said Mrs. Stodart. 'It's dangerous. Could catch in anything.'

'Give up, Mother. I like it like that. Looks great to see it streaming in the wind. Anyway, if it is that rough she will have a hat on.'

The race was cancelled, but they were kitted out for any eventuality – wet suits, sailing boots, overalls, life jackets. And sure enough when the tide turned the wind started to smash into it. White horses riding on the tops of the waves were being blown sickeningly apart to disappear as spindrift in the air. The boats barged as they strove to free themselves from torment.

'Two are off!' shouted Fergus as he and Scud ran for the flat, rubber rescue boat.

'Move it,' growled the Coxswain already with the engine revved up to leave the pier.

With a dash that cleaved a white sided, curved furrow and stood the craft on edge, they threw themselves towards the stricken boats now drifting side-on towards the sandbanks in their path.

'Get me on that farthest one!' yelled Scud.

They moved alongside the helpless craft, but bouncing and banging alongside they failed to get a rope aboard until Scud threw himself on deck.

'Get the other one and come back for me. I'll get an anchor down.'

Leaving Scud sprawled precariously on the cabin roof Fergus and the Coxswain set off toward the second boat. For some capricious reason, a mere 50 metres off to starboard, the second boat lay meekly in a trough. Fergus stepped aboard with ease and had the engine firing moments later.

But just as things seemed in control a knife-edged cry tore the air apart.

'Fe-e-rrie!' Scud instinctively cried as he crashed headlong into the sea.

He had been thrown overboard and dashed against the hull. His arm was smashed and although the others could not know that scream was quite enough. Fergus jumped from deck to rubber duck and swiftly with the coxswain got to him fast and on his way to shore.

The floundering boat was left to take its chances as Fergus sought medical aid for Scud. From then the Stodarts could but wait and worry.

Would Scud's life be spared and would his arm ever be the same again? To make sure he lived was clearly foremost in their minds, but nagging and persistent was the thought: "Could a one armed sailor sail?"

Chapter 35 Scud is injured

Scud was in a bad way.

The ambulance, ringing its strident tone, rushed him through the streets to doctors who fought to save his life.

At home, when all that could be done was done, the family were worried sick. Fergus, in anguish, called down the heavens upon his head.

'I never should have let him go on that boat,' he groaned, 'but he was too quick for me. You know what he's like. He was on board before I could move. I'll no' forgive myself.'

'It's not your fault, Fergus,' said Mairi. 'That's what makes him great. He'll pull through.'

'But will he sail again? If he can't sail, I dunno. . . . He'll maybe never make it. He's got to make it, He's better than me, you know. He's better than any of us. He's great. God! What are we going to do? We can't just sit and watch.'

'He'll be all right,' said Mairi.

'I can't see any change. He's just lying in that bed. We've got to do something.'

'Fergus, we don't know how to cure people. We just have to go and see him every day. They say that'll help.'

'I know what'll cure him,' said Pete. 'Get Christiana to visit him.'

'Hells Teeth!' shouted Fergus, 'and how do we do that?'

'It's a thought though,' said Mairi. 'That could work. Does anybody know how to reach her?'

'Nah,' said Fergus. 'We never knew. We never even saw the Helix when we found it, never mind her.'

'It had a lot to do with stone circles,' said Pete. 'Is there one near here?

'Not one that I'd go near,' said Mairi. 'There's the two through the Pillars but I can't see us getting through again without Scud. . . sorry Fergus. Wait a minute there's that old Priory at Cromlech. I think that name means stone circle. I bet there's one there.'

‘Right!’ said Fergus forcefully. ‘Let’s find it and get that woman here.’

Chapter 36 Loch of the Spirits

The need to act consumed their every thought.

Scud lay still and broken encased in white and the time to act was now.

'Mairi,' said Fergus. 'Have you any idea where this place is?'

'It's south of here – on an island – in the "Loch of the Spirits".'

'The Spirits,' bellowed an overwrought Fergus. 'Oh my God! Still that's probably the place to go to contact someone who's 700 hundred years old.'

'I've read about it,' said Pete. 'It's in the Strath. We could cycle there – it's maybe 45 kilometres.'

'Right, Pete,' said Fergus. 'Tell us about it. What's it like?'

'That's about all I know. Mairi, you must know. Remember, you said it was a good book – "The Rider of the Storm" or something.'

'Oh yeah. That one. The loch is long and narrow and the wind and spray that's whipped up is supposed to be the anger of the "Spirit" that lives there. There's an old ruined Priory on the island that's been built on the site of an old Celtic temple. I'm not sure about a stone circle but that's about the gist of it.'

'Never mind a circle for now. It sounds like the kind of place to find Christiana. It's Thursday. We'll go tomorrow. We'll just tell Mum and Dad we have to get away camping for the weekend, but that we'll go in to see Scud before we leave. They'll understand.'

'Fergus,' said Mairi, 'arrangements? Tents, sleeping bags, food and how are we to get across to the island? We can't take the Osprey.'

'Ah, right, a blow up. Nah, we are not going across a loch like that in a rubber bath. Canoes, that's it. You know that man – the great tall one – that's got the outdoor centre? He's got good, inflatable canoes. One will do. Pete, you know him. Tonight, borrow one and a pump and all of us – pack a life jacket and sailing gear. Mairi, food, anything. Stick it in a haversack and bring it. I'll get anything else.'

As usual, the parents only got half the story – no mention of spirits or 700 year old girls.

By the next night, they were off and by eight o'clock they were camped by the side of the "Loch of the Spirits". The area was beautiful and thickly covered with trees of birch and ash. The shore had grass down to the edge of the loch except where here and there the turf had been torn away to form neat little gravel beaches.

Off-shore, the island, bathed in moonlight, glistened ominously showing up ruined buildings and walls as the likely home of the spirits of the loch.

'Bed now,' said Mairi 'and over to the island first thing in the morning.'

Chapter 37 They find the Centre of the Circle

In the morning, all was changed.

The island clothed in forest greenery looked lush and fresh, a haven for a noble building, ruined but majestic in its setting.

'Spirits!' roared Fergus. 'There are no spirits here. Christiana will never come.'

'It's cool,' said Mairi.

'Maybe the Spirit only comes at night,' said Pete. 'Looks different.'

'Well, let's get ready and go over,' said Mairi. 'It doesn't matter about the Spirit. It's Christiana we're trying to reach.'

The journey was easy in the long, inflated canoe. They cut through the sparkling water with ease and landed just below the Priory. With the canoe hauled up and camp made, they formed their plan,

Mairi took charge. 'Right, we're looking for a stone circle – might be any size – but we better go to the Priory first. Look for a circular wall. There's likely. . . What's happening. It's freezing. . . . It's going dark!'

Suddenly, the atmosphere had changed: The sun had died and the waters of the loch were being whipped up and sprayed like icy bullets.

'There's something wrong,' shouted Pete. 'Take cover.'

They ran to the Priory and cowered behind a wall. Wind and water lashed the building and in a flash their paradise had descended into hell.

'It must be the Spirit,' said a shaken Mairi. 'It doesn't like us being here.'

'Give over,' said Fergus. 'It's just a weather front going through. It'll clear.'

'Well maybe,' said Mairi cautiously, 'but if a 700 year old can come and help Scud, something else that doesn't like us can disagree,'

Then it all changed again. The sun came out, the water calmed down and all was serene.

‘That was a warning,’ said Mairi. ‘Be careful. Don’t upset anything.’

‘Yeah, yeah,’ growled Fergus. ‘I wish I had been careful enough to bring waterproofs. That would have been more like it. It’s a circular wall we want is it?’

‘Yes, but go carefully. Shout if you find stones with strange signs on them and yell if you find more upright stones with another on top like before.’

‘They climbed through weed-ridden rooms where the roofs had fallen in, along passages and into little outdoor squares with statues and stone benches, before coming on a massive wall that once must have been part of an important place of worship. But there were no stone circles.

And then at a fallen tree, Pete called, ‘Look at this.’

A tree when it fell had sprung up a plat of roots at right angles to the ground. Here and there the roots had threaded through a bank of stones which showed signs of human building and there was enough to show that this was a circular wall. They stared at it until it dawned what they were looking at.’

‘Well done, Pete. This could be it,’ said Mairi.

And almost right away, but a little further on, they came on a double bank of stones laid in the same curve.

‘I’m telling you, this is it,’ said Mairi – ‘a stone circle buried beneath a Celtic temple. What we need now is the centre. Fergus, join up the two walls in a curve with your rope.’

When this was done, she said, ‘now we go in at right angles to that curve.’

‘Fergus, you try and walk right round the curve until you are opposite us. Somewhere between us, in the middle, we should find something - maybe a kind of stool like the last time. And look out for stones with signs on them.’

Fergus moved around, but they lost him just as he was about to come in line.

‘Where are you, Fergus?’ shouted Mairi. ‘I can’t see you.’

‘I’m right opposite, I think, but it’s dark in here and I’m bang up against that big wall.’

'Hold on. We'll try and reach you,' said Mairi.

The light that made it past the stones and branches showed up things in black and white. The growth that curled round their feet made movement a stumbling shambles. It was a world apart and took every bit of courage that they had. They pushed on toward the centre.

'Can you see him, Pete?'

'Nope, he's still behind that wall.'

'We'll try and reach the wall and then see where he is.'

The three of them almost met at the wall, Fergus on one side and Mairi and Pete on the other.

'Fergus!' shouted Mairi. 'This wall is no' a wall. It's a giant stone.' Go round the left hand side, reach through with your arm and we'll pull you.'

Covered with earth and scratched and torn, Fergus emerged very relieved to see the other two.

'I thought I was trapped in there. Some place this.'

'Look at this stone,' said Pete. 'It's got something sticking out the top and there on the face, it's writing.'

'They're church signs,' said Mairi. 'That thing at the top could be a cross with a side broken off and there's the outline of a huge cross right down the face. This is probably the centre of the Priory.'

'Can't be,' said Pete. 'There's the sun-god. That circle with a face in it and wavy lines sticking out of it – that's pagan.'

'It is the centre,' said Mairi. 'It's the very centre of the Priory and the ancient stone circle. See there at the foot of the stone – an old tree trunk with a flat top. There would have been a stone on it once. That is from the original stone circle altar. And in front of it, a cut stone one – that's the Priory. An ancient stone circle has been taken over and made a Priory.'

'We're there,' she said.

Chapter 38 The Wheel of Light

But could they contact Christiana?

How could they tell if she would come for them? She would come for Scud but would she come for them.

They camped on island soil and the following day they gathered quietly round the tree trunk altar.

'Do we say anything?' said Pete.

'How would we know?' said Fergus. 'I'm no' going to stand here and say "Abracadabra". '

'No.' said Mairi. 'We just stand here and say, Hello Christiana. Can you hear us? Either she can or she can't. Come on, we've come this far. Concentrate. We'll sit round the altar and I'll ask first. Still, maybe you should, Fergus. Maybe she fancies you as well.'

'Nah, not me. She's Scud's girl. Even I have got that message.'

'Okay,' said Mairi. 'Here we go. Christiana, can you hear me? Scud's been hurt. He's in hospital and he's very ill and he needs your help.'

And at that moment the wind howled through the trees; the temperature dropped; and they could hear gales whipping up the waters of the loch. It lasted only a minute or two and everything was quiet again.

'Something is telling us something,' said Pete nervously.

'Okay, try again, Mairi,' said Fergus. 'We can't sit around here all day.'

'Christiana, can you hear me? Scud's been hurt. He's been hurt badly and he needs your help.'

Mairi's eyes grew large and round because before her was a ring of fire, a wheel of fire and at its centre, a face.

'It's Christiana, Mairi – but I see your eyes are filled with dread. Do not be afraid for it will not last. I had trouble getting through and when that happens I end up like this.'

The flames quickly left her body and the light in which she was encased died down. It left a Christiana in regal garb because she came as Queen – as Christiana of the Isles.

'You're beautiful, Christiana. I only knew from Scud and you are everything he said you were.'

'And so are you although I have seen you before. Your golden hair falls down your back like a daughter of the Cuch. I know you sail with skill and are clever beyond compare. In my land you would be a Princess of my House.'

'Alas, it is dangerous for us to meet. I only reached you because you have a hair of Scud upon your clothing. The Spirit of this place allows me to contact only one and that person is Lord Scud who is ennobled in my land. We must make haste.'

'Yes, Christiana. Scud is badly injured. He fell trying to stave off a shipwreck. Will you go to him?'

'Yes Mairi, but I must leave this instant for fear the Spirit of this place loses patience and sends the water to swamp this circle and all within it.'

* * *

'Try again, Mairi,' said Fergus, 'and then that's it. We'll try something else. We've got to think of something that works.'

'She's been. I've told her.'

'What!' exploded Fergus. 'Not again. I keep traipsing about all over the country and I never see sight or sign of her. You're not at it as well, are you?'

'No, she's really only allowed to contact Scud. Things are difficult for her as well. She was on fire when she got here.'

'Where did all this happen? We were standing right next to you. I never saw a fire. Did you see a fire, Pete? No. You didn't?'

'Mairi,' said Pete. 'I'll believe you if you tell me it's true, but. . . I don't know what to believe.'

'It's true.' She's off to see Scud now. If she hadn't left in a hurry the Spirit of the Loch would have swamped the whole island. We better get out of here.'

'God only knows what's happening,' said Fergus. 'Let's go.'

They scrambled out, packed and took off in their long canoe. They had not far to go, but from the west and unseen by them, a belt of cloud, black and menacing, bore down on the loch. Their dipping paddles worked up to speed and they left the shore fast until the water rose, surged and broke in front of them. Their canoe lunged from side to side as Fergus despairingly tried to steer a course.

They filled with water and as Mairi and Pete turned to bail their speed slackened to a crawl.

'No,' screamed Fergus. 'Pete, keep paddling. Mairi, bail.'

The surface was a turbulent mess of spray and icy, slashing streams of water. The canoe twice put its nose beneath the water and twice almost threw them in until with the bow up in the air, a wave – and who gets waves on an inland loch – hit it underneath. With a crash all three and all they possessed hurtled into the water.

It looked like the end for swimming to the shore was surely beyond their human means. But as they surfaced it was as if a giant hand came down and swept the water flat. The wind dropped and the water calmed.

They swam the last few metres to the shore and with them came their gear. Their canoe, as gentle as could be and with scarce a sound nosed in to lie up on the gravel beach.

'We certainly got kicked out of there,' said a battered Fergus.

'We did,' said Mairi sadly but not displeased.

Pete was exhausted and had no breath left to say anything.

They cycled home that night. Fergus was confused, but Mairi knew that all would now be well and vowed to help Scud become the greatest sailor in the land. Pete put his trust in her.

They reached home to find their Mum and Dad, relaxed, aglow and full of life. 'You will never believe this,' said Mrs Stodart. 'The hospital has just phoned to say that Scud has recovered consciousness, wants up and is definitely on the mend.' It's a miracle,' she said.

Chapter 39 The Race

Scud soon recovered.

His recuperation amazed his family and his friends. In spite of an arm broken in two places and unconscious for three days. when he awoke he was on his feet as soon as he could balance.'

'Talk about magic,' said Fergus. 'I don't know what we were worried about. Did you just want to get your head down for a few days?'

'No, I saw you, I think, when I was out, but I couldn't move. Maybe I didn't actually see you. I don't know.'

'You were out cold - couldn't see you for bandages. Is your arm going to be all right? You'll need that.'

'You weren't great, Scud,' said Mairi. 'We were worried.'

'All I can remember is thinking of Christiana and there she was.'

The three of them looked at each other, but no-one said anything about the "Spirit of the Loch".

'What did she say?' said Mairi.

'Not a lot. She did something, I think. Don't know what. It's all a bit hazy.'

'She did say, "Get better, you'll get better" and I did. It was great seeing her again.'

The sailing season was drawing to a close and Scud's arm was still in plaster.

'How am I going to sail with this lump on my arm?'

If he said it once he said it a hundred times until everyone was fed up hearing it. Actually he had been out with Mairi, but he had to crew and that was no longer for him.

'I want to sail in the last race – the Commodore's Junior Burgee and I certainly can't do it like this.'

'When do you see the Doctor again?'

'Monday.'

'If the plaster comes off that'll give you twelve days to practise before the Burgee.'

'Yes, if it is taken off. And I've got to do something about thanking Christiana now that you've told me what actually happened. She's never been back, but she'll be busy now that she is definitely Queen.'

'You can get in touch with her and thank her, can you?'

'I'm not sure.'

Mairi had eventually told Scud of their adventures while trying to reach Christiana but no-one, not even Scud, wanted to upset that Spirit again.

'There are her brothers; I expect they're still making trouble. Maybe she needs help with them. I'd like to go there and see what I can do. Bet I could sail a fighting boat for her.'

'Scud, get real. You want to go and live 700 years ago and fight for her. You're a good sailor, but you are not very old. Anyway I thought you said you had decided not to go,'

'Temporarily. I don't see why we shouldn't be able to travel to each other's time. That would solve some of our problems. We can't really be close unless we can.'

That Monday, Scud got the plaster off and his arm was fine.

'Tonight, Mairi. Training?'

'Can't tonight. I've got a load of work. It's October and the exams are in November or don't you care. Anyway, it'll be dark.'

'We can sail in the dark.'

'Well, maybe in front of the clubhouse to get your eye in again. We'll practise round the mooring buoys.'

And they did. They could see enough to sail a kind of sausage course between two buoys and it was very skilful work. They went round the buoy at either end, leaning right and left, to weave a course going in wide to exit with the buoy almost on board or in to miss by an inch and leave it wide and free. They threw their weight and swung the boat as tight as on a sloping track to leave them hurtling up the course with speed.

'You're fine,' said Mairi. 'Timing's good and co-ordination's groovy We'll do all right.'

'What about tomorrow?'

‘No, Scud. I’m busy, but I’ll do an hour right after school on Thursday seeing you’ve been ill. And then we’ll do the whole weekend. There’s no race so we’ll get Pete and Fergus to join us.’

The two were ready for the race and nothing was going to baulk them of the flag.

That Saturday fifteen boats came up for battle. Scud tangled with his brothers from the start and the two boats sailed into the line with Scud to turn into the rival boat and force it off its course.

He did it slowly and in accordance with the rules, but suddenly, as Fergus turned away to avoid a crash, he pulled in sail, swung back and left his brothers for dead.

‘My God!’ said Mr Stodart watching his sons joust like knights, ‘I know “luffing up” is allowed even at the start but Fergus will be furious.’ And so he might because as the gun boomed, Scud and Mairi were clean away.

They took the lead with Fergus and Pete in fourth but chasing hard. By leg four, Fergus was lying second but still ten metres off the lead. Try as he might he could not catch his younger brother – ten metres is a massive lead in anybody’s language.

Leg after leg, Fergus stayed in second position and behind his younger brother. Then, as Scud and Mairi were coming off the beat to launch themselves into the run, Scud called for the balloon-shaped spinnaker a shade too early. Up it went and while they were still broadside to the wind it filled and set the boat on edge.

In an instant, Scud and Mairi threw themselves out to tilt the hovering boat back on an even keel. For a micro-second, which seemed like an age, it stuck. If the boat fell flat their race was over. If it swung back, they still had a chance,

With a mighty slap the boat came right, and amidst a drenching downpour of water from the sails, they set their boat in order and prepared to take up the chase.

To cries and whoops of glee, a triumphant Fergus and a jubilant Pete had flown past at speed to take the lead.

Scud and Mairi were now fourth.

Chapter 40 Genius or Genes.

'We need a miracle now,' said Mairi.

'A miracle!' shouted Scud. 'I'll settle for the wind staying steady.'

The wind blew fast and slow. One minute blowing them along and then disappearing to leave them at the mercy of the tide.

'Get that spinnaker down,' said Scud. 'We'll goosewing now. Quick, get the jib on the other side. The spinnaker's too finicky.'

'We're the only ones without a spinnaker up,' said Mairi worried at the move.

'The wind's too fluky and it's going to swing again. A sail out either side will be better. You'll see.'

It did and their steady pace took in the first three whose progress was a thing of stops and starts. The leg was long and gave them the chance to be a threat again. Ten metres from the buoy that marked the final leg the wind struck hard and all four had yet to make the turn.

'Hold on, Mairi,' said Scud, 'here's our chance. Get ready to gybe. Get Ready. Gybe Oh'. He pushed the tiller away from him, the boom crashed over; they ducked underneath it, balanced the boat and turned it tight round the buoy and inside the other three. They were in the lead.

'I didn't think that was possible in that wind,' said Mairi. 'Look at the other three. They're away out to port. They didn't go round that way.'

'Mairi, I hate to say it, but concentrate. We're in the lead and your jib is backing.'

Shaken by such a move a desperate Fergus abandoned caution. He sailed headlong after Scud and diced on the line between safety and disaster. The boat baulked and reared and stood on end and water slewed from bow to stern.

Pete, hanging over the side trying to keep the boat level had to dive inboard as one lurch after another threatened to dump him overboard. Eventually one wrong move ended it all and Pete plunged headfirst into the sea.

'NO,' shouted Mrs Stodart on the shore. 'He'll leave him. He'll never stop as long as Scud's out front.'

But right is right and Fergus, no matter how he felt, left the battle, came into the wind and picked up Pete.

Scud and Mairi crossed the line to take the winner's gun.

'Are you sure Christiana's not in this boat?' said Mairi. 'There has to be some explanation for what you just did.'

'No, the thanks go all to you. Bit hairy though.'

'That's the end of sailing for a bit, though I'll have to try and contact Christiana if I'm ever going to thank her. But how?'

'I thought you knew about stone circles. I wouldn't try at the Loch of the Spirit though. We're not popular.'

'I've heard there are local ones,' said Scud 'and there's the statue outside the village.'

'Go to the library or Mr Turner at the museum,' said Mairi. 'Or ask, Pete.'

'I'll ask at the library. I don't think I'll be too popular with Pete at the moment.'

And sure enough there was a nearer one and an elated Scud hurried home to tell Mairi of his find.

'There's a circle near here at Clada – that's only five miles away.'

'Are you sure? I've never heard of it.'

'Yes, it's called Druidtemple.'

'Ah!' said Mairi, 'The Standing Stones of Clada. That's not a Circle.'

'It was, but there are only five stones left.'

'Scud, don't go there. That's a terrible place.'

'I'll to go the village stone first, but I've got to reach her.'

'Well, if you do go, don't go at night and don't walk three times round the big stone. If you do, the Devil will get you – not Christiana. Least that's what they say. I better come with you.'

'No, I've got to go and it has to be alone. You know that.'

He looked at her – 'and I'm going now.'

Chapter 41 The Fangs of Boreas

That night Christiana was not at the village stone and Scud left to try the local circle.

Clada was known in the village and tales were told in awe and fear. It was the place where sacrifices had been made to long forgotten gods; where stones were marked with signs and cup like holes that told of fearful deeds; and where at mid-day the winter sun came in to lose its weak and flickering life.

Scud soon reached the broken circle and could see that it had once been a mighty place; that even now massive stones stood up in solitary splendour almost defying time to take away their power. He was not scared, but sensible enough to recognise the force that this place held as he walked toward the nearest of the stones.

Standing before a three metre giant he simply asked, 'Christiana, can you hear me? Can you come?'

He asked but once and there she was.

'Stand still, Scud,' she said. 'Get out of this place now.'

'We've got to talk, Christiana,' said Scud cautiously. 'Thanks for helping me at the hospital.'

'Scud, what are you doing here. This is a dangerous place. GET OUT! If it was midnight I could not save you.'

'But a stone circle is the only place I can call you.'

'Do not use this one again. These are Devil stones. Get out now,' she shrieked. 'I'll meet you at the stone outside your village. Walk away slowly but not round this stone and do not look back.'

Scud found his bike and set off home. He had hardly gone a hundred metres when streams of fury cracked across the sky. Coloured lights – blue, green, rose and violet - streamed above his head. With a crash a curtain of light with two 'V' shaped jagged edges zoomed down to disappear somewhere behind him.

It left him marooned in darkness: No sound, no light and just an eerie sense of something lost. He shivered as blackness filled up the ground along the road like some great cavern with neither an opening nor an exit. Then up ahead he made out the white breakers of the sea. Instantly he relaxed. He knew the sea and when he reached its shore he would be safe.

He got home to find a worried Mairi. 'You look like you've seen a ghost I've been waiting ages for you. What happened?'

'I don't know. Christiana came and told me to get out of the circle fast.'

'I told you it was horrible.'

'I've to meet her at the village stone. She wasn't there the last time.'

'Are you all right?'

'I'm here but I'm not all right. I got attacked.'

'You got attacked,' said Fergus coming up behind them. 'Who attacked you?'

'Something came out of the sky. A forked tongue just missed me and somebody was throwing huge fireworks – coloured lights and bombs bursting all over he place.'

'You've got him then,' said Pete.' I heard the last bit. We were attacked coming back from the island but this sounds worse, Where were you anyway?'

'The Druidtemple'

'Clada! You didn't go to Clada.'

'I went to see Christiana but she threw me off.'

'You're nuts. Fancy going to the Druidtemple at night.'

'Mairi, what is this?' interrupted Fergus. 'I know something odd happened at the loch, but you know as well as I do that he saw the Northern Lights, that's all. They're great. I saw them last year.'

'It's not great when you're trying to get out of Clada,' said Scud.

'No, it's not,' said Mairi 'The Aurora Borealis is its real name, but I don't think Boreas was very nice.'

'For Heavens Sake!' said Fergus 'who have we got now? I wish you would stick to sailing, Scud.'

'I've never heard of Boreas. Christiana has never mentioned him to me,' said Scud. 'It's not my fault.'

'Boreas is the North Wind,' said Marie. 'He wrecks ships and things. You don't want to get on the wrong side of him.'

'The lights that disappeared behind you, Scud,' said Pete. 'V-shaped lines?'

'Yeah, two.'

'Boreas has two serpent's feet like fangs.'

'Aw, chuck it you two,' said Fergus. 'Scud I'm you're big brother and your ex-skipper. Go and find Christiana and stick with her. One ghost's enough for anybody.'

'What are you all wandering about for at this time of night, anyway,' said Scud.

'Wandering about!' said Fergus sarcastically. 'Everybody has been looking for you. Mum's worried sick. Go and tell her you got lost in the dark or something.'

'Yes, Scud,' said Marie. 'You can find Christiana tomorrow.'

Chapter 42 The Dolmetron

Scud was at the stone early next morning.

There was no sign of Christiana but eventually, looking tired and troubled, she turned up. 'It's not easy getting through here sometimes and I've got problems at home.'

'Not your brothers again.'

'Yes, but are you all right?'

'Yeah, Boreas tried his tricks on the way home, but nothing too bad. Christiana, this is ridiculous. I couldn't live permanently in your world and you have to be in your kingdom a lot. Why can't I travel back and forward like you?'

'It is difficult, Scud. You know the state I get into sometimes trying to get through. And anyway you need a Dolmetron. Without one I would never get here. It works quite well through a stone circle but getting back is a problem. I kind of bounce back and I can never stay long. You have not got one.'

'Where did you get it from?'

'Oh, we did not build it. It was made long ago – maybe thousands of years ago.'

'How do you aim it?'

'You do not aim it. You stand underneath it when the wind blows into it. It has to blow fast, very fast and you cannot be sure where you will end up.'

'But you always get here.'

'The first time I came, I could not be sure where I would end up. I was desperate and I took a chance. I had heard a story that my Aunt Jane managed it and we now know that she did.'

'And you never go anywhere else?'

'Not now. I made sure when we first met. You can go to where you have left a piece of your body so I left a piece of my hair under your village stone. Some stone circles work a different way, but I'm not exactly sure how. It's usually rougher but quicker.'

'A body part. Ugh. You sure hair will do? A body part, that's blood and everything.'

'Yes, hair does fine.'

'I don't know, Christiana. It's scary. Does it always work?'

'It's called "entanglement." It moves you fast through time. It'll even work with another person if you exchange body parts.'

'What?' shouted Scud.

'Scud, that is what a blood brother is. But it is dangerous and there is a lot I do not know yet.'

'I'll learn and I'll leave a bit of hair here so that I can come back.'

'But a Dolmetron - you do not have one as far as I know. You have stone circles, but I have never heard of a Dolmetron here. 'Scud, I will have to get back. If I do not go, I will never get back.'

'I don't even know what one looks like.'

'It can be like a stool but big or it can have one leg and have a mushroom shaped cap on top. Two upright stones have a third one balanced on top. There are a lot of stones built up like this, but to be a Dolmetron all the stones have to be magnetic. When the top stone wobbles or spins it rises and something happens. If you stand under it when it is like this you are transported.'

'Are you sure about this body business? They used to cut people up on stones like these, you know.'

'Yes, but hair will do. Scud, I must go.'

'I'll find one,' shouted Scud as she disappeared

* * *

'Mairi, I need to find a very, very, windy valley,' said Scud.

'A valley with a lot of wind - they're everywhere. Take your pick.'

'It has to have a lot of Standing Stones, as well.'

'Ditto,' said Mairi. 'What is this, Scud?'

'If I tell you will you promise not to tell anyone else? - not even Fergus and Pete.'

'If it has to do with Christiana, Fergus is the last person to tell. Mind, as long as he doesn't think it is one of your stories, he can be a great help.'

'No, this would be hopeless if other people knew. Even you knowing makes it difficult. Least I think so.'

'Thanks a bunch but I don't want to know. If it helps I promise not to tell.'

'Christiana gets here using something called a Dolmetron that can shift you to a different time.'

'You're right. Fergus will go ballistic with that one.'

Scud told Mairi everything he knew about it.

'Are you saying that she cuts off a bit off herself so that she can meet you.'

'Yes, but a piece of hair will do and I don't think she needs to do that with a stone circle. It's very complicated and even she doesn't understand it all.'

'I'm not surprised,' said Mairi.

'Will you help me find a windy valley with standing stones?'

Mairi knew that strange things had happened and not understanding was no reason to say he had been dreaming or that it was one of his stories.

'I've heard of the Valley of the Stones. It's out west somewhere and I suppose it could be windy. I'm sure it will be out there specially on an island.'

'We'll have to go there and check,' said Scud.

'Scud, you've got to promise me you won't suddenly disappear. I can't go home and say you are off to the 14th century.'

'No, I won't.'

'And you're sure this isn't some kind of Druid's ceremony or something? Count me out if it is.'

'No, Mairi, I told you. A piece of hair will do,'

They were now into something buried deep in time. The forces sought were huge and often filled with dread. Tales were told of stones that walked; of those that had a pact with the sun and moon to make mankind their slaves; and of disobedient souls who had their bodies turned to stone. They were into dangerous practices.

'I don't see how we can go off to the West Coast on our own,' said Mairi. 'It's too far. What would we tell the others? Mum and Dad would have something to say.'

'How far is it?' said Scud.

'Far enough. We'd need a lift in a car, a boat and certainly Fergus and Pete.'

'Not yet. I'd feel daft telling them till I can prove it.'

'How then?'

'Don't know. I'll think of something.'

Chapter 43 Valley of the Stones

There was only one way.

Scud knew he could not do it on his own and he dare not tell his brothers of his plan. He trusted Mairi with the secret, but feared to involve her in his search. There was only one who knew it was all true and who could also sail him to the Valley of the Stones.

'Mairi, I'm going to speak to Christiana. She'll take me in her boat.'

'She can get her boat here as well?'

'She's done it before.'

A baffled and weary Mairi shrugged and trailed off home. She loved her brother and knew he was special. She was sure he did not tell her lies, but sometimes he pushed her to the edge of understanding and doubts began to creep into her troubled mind.

Scud cycled straight to Clada. The dangers of the Devil-haunted place were clear and vivid in his mind, but nothing, not a scary thought or a fleeting doubt stopped him in his quest. Anyway, he told himself, it's not midnight and I'm just going in and out.

Sure enough Christiana appeared but in a fury.

'You idiot! You are here again.'

'It's important, Christiana. I need. . .'

'QUIET! If it is that important go to the village stone, NOW. I will get there as soon as I can get through to it.'

Scud cycled to the stone outside his village and lay down at the side of the bay to wait for Christiana. The water shimmered and glistened in the moonlight and cast shadows all around. It was mysterious and wonderful and it was home.

He opened up his eyes and there she was. 'You're here,' was all he trusted himself to say to this figure whose noble bearing set off with golden tiara and a fur trimmed purple open robe proclaimed her as the Queen.

'Yes, but I wish, nay I command that you do not come again to the Devil's Temple. There will be another near.'

'I was in a hurry. I've found a likely place for a Dolmetron – The Valley of the Stones.'

'Where is that?' said Christiana.

'Out west, it's on an island. I don't know the exact position yet.'

'Ah. "Glennnan na Clash. I've heard of it. There is a Dolmetron there?'

'Probably. Can you get me there?'

'Yes, I can and we will go now.'

'Now. Will it take long?'

'No, we will go right down the Great Glen, up past Mull and into the open sea. The island-Goath – lies somewhere beyond Ard na Murchan'

'You can't sail right down the Great Glen,' said Scud.

'I can,' said Christiana.' You must have patience, my Lord Scud,' using the accolade she conferred on him when they last sailed on her boat.

In front of Scud, rocking gently in the waters of the bay was the Christiana's Dragon craft, with its fearsome head rearing up above the bow and almost breathing fire.

'Come on board and take your place by my right side.'

'My Lady,' said the warrior at the tiller, 'will the Lord Scud accept a robe?'

'I'm sure he should,' said Lady Christiana. 'He is hardly dressed for sailing far less for any kind of action should we encounter any opposition to our plans.'

The huge, rangy, hairy man of war appeared savage and unkempt. Weapons sprouted from his back, his waist, his side and he left no doubt he knew how to use them.

And yet – Scud paused for thought – beneath the fearsome image lay a princely guise. He wore a coat of burnished mail and a helmet inlaid with gold. And on his arms where muscles bulged, gold bands shone even in the fitful light. His weapons, although showing signs of frequent use, were not those of any ordinary man.

A warrior and helmsman – a chief – he was the man called "Finn of the Swords" and he used these weapons ferociously in

Christiana's cause. A man with scarce a moment except for her and those who fought bravely by her side.

And here he was acknowledging the place of Scud by Christiana's side. He offered a surcoat of leather trimmed with fur and belted to hold it tight in battle and on the sea. On his Queen's command and with studied grace he assisted Scud to don the garment. A leather cap with bars of silver back and front was placed upon his head and he assumed his place amongst these folk.

The boat was full of sailors: Men for rowing, men for bailing, those who stood by ropes to raise and swing the sail and important men to steer.

At first, moving slowly, the boat edged out into the stream and soon the oars, dipping with the grace of wings, gave them the power they needed.

Round the point and heading west the wind took them from the stern.

The big, square sail was hauled up the mast and billowed forward to set the boat on charge. Swaying purposefully but in control, it cleaved through the built up waves. Water spumed up in arcs of white and crashed down along the sides to leave a trail that gave credence to its power.

A Dragon leant forward snarling aggression in every line of its terrible, monstrous head.

'Now for this island,' said Christiana.

Chapter 44 Island of Goath

They were headed for the Western Isles and only Finn knew where it lay. It was a very small, insignificant place almost lost in the myriad of islands on the Atlantic Seaboard. It was not all that far and, once round the point of Ard na Murchan, Finn soon had them drawing up upon its shore. Morning was breaking with the sun slowly coming up behind them when they set foot on its sands.

'Where do we go from here?' said Scud.

'We will follow that stream,' said Christiana. 'It will go through a valley somewhere.'

Leaving Finn as custodian of the boat, Christiana, Scud and two crew members to act as guards worked their way up the hill. When the trees began to thin they saw the cleft. The slopes had parted to form an opening about 20 metres wide and facing the sea. Even from far off they saw the standing stones they sought, some upright, some lying flat. On a bank raised above the others, monumental and imposing, were what looked like several ancient structures.

One was like a giant mushroom with an upright stem capped by a large, roundish stone. Another was like the giant stool that Scud was looking for, but with an extra slab set within it and seemingly standing free. This centre slab was pierced to form a circular hole worked right through and ground and rubbed until its sides were silk-like to the touch. The structures, set to face the sea, were huge and made of brownish-red, black-streaked rock.

'It is made of lodestone,' said Christiana.

'Lodestone?' said Scud.

'A Dolmetron' is made of lodestone and we use it to navigate when it is cloudy. If you float it, it always points north.'

'How do you float a rock?'

'A small piece and tie it to a cork.'

'A compass!' said Scud.

'Never mind what it is called, it is handy sometimes, but I prefer the stars and the sun – safer. This is probably a Dolmetron though but my one is completely black. I do not know about the hole.'

'It's used for something,' said Scud. 'It has been bored deliberately and it is pointing at the mushroom thing.'

'There is no wind so there will be nothing to see until there is,' said Christiana. 'The cap has to move before it can rise.'

When the wind came they saw. It whistled through the hole and forced the cap to quiver: immediately it rose to hover in the air.

'Get back. Back.' shouted a fearful Christiana.' Back or who knows where we will end up. It works though, but how? It is not all that windy.'

'It's the hole – the venturi effect,' said Scud.

'Venturi, what's venturi?'

'We use it in sailing. 'I've got two sails. You squeeze the wind between them and it speeds up. That's what the hole's for.'

'Amazing. Makes you go faster does it?'

'No bother. When I come to your place I'll show you?'

* * *

'Scud, what are you doing lying here?' said Mairi.

'Oh, I'm back. Great,' he said as he rose from the bank at the side of the bay.

'I've been with Christiana. We found a Dolmetron on Goath and it works. But I'm sorry, Mairi. I said I wouldn't go away suddenly and then Christiana appeared and we sailed to the island. What did you tell Mum?'

'Tell Mum. You went out of the house about an hour ago. I'm not even looking for you. But it's nonsense this time. You're making it up. You can't have been out west. It would take days.'

'I did, I tell you. I sailed to that island. I'll show you the Dolmetron, if you'll come.'

Chapter 45 They Telescope Time

He had to contact Christiana again.

It was getting easier all the time, but even he was surprised by the speed of her response,‘

‘Are you all right?’

‘Yes, but I want to come to where you are - just for a while.’

‘Are you sure?’

‘Yeah, we can bury hair at both Dolmetrons and the Stone and go between the two places whenever we want, can’t we?’

‘We have not proved your one works yet but probably, yes. I’m not sure how often we could do this but we’ll see.’

‘What about getting to Goath quickly?’

‘That is a problem. I am sure it is possible. My cousin Angus Og showed me a few things like that, but we might disappear into the stars. I’ll think about it.’

An excited Scud was floating on air. It was all happening. His absences were never noticed and it was as if he had never been away. The two worlds had different time scales.

Life went on. He had a lot to do on the boats. Fergus had started up winter work to prepare them for racing in the spring. Scud was also asked to demonstrate the art of gybing to the younger sailors in the club. A difficult manoeuvre, it often conjured up feelings of dread and fear. For him this turning of the boat with the wind behind; the sudden rush of power; and the slamming of the boom from side to side held no such fears. He had perfected motion, balance, and a system which turned terror into grace.

In this world of sail his genius was emerging fast, a prince about to claim his throne. His time was fully taken up. His days were full and yet there gnawed away the thought that in that other world, where already dubbed a prince, he had yet to prove his worth. He had to go.

He called on Christiana again and her Dragon craft appeared on the waters of the bay.

'I want to come back with you, I'm ready. I'll help to fight your battles and with Finn of the Swords I'll finish off those who harm your position in Garmoran.'

'For good?'

'No, I'll have to be back for the beginning of the sailing season. You could come back with me and be plain Christiana again.'

'I might, but my kingdom is at war and I durst not leave it long.'

They set off right away for Goath – Finn at the tiller and Scud standing proudly by Christiana's side upon the prow.

'Do you always command from here?' said Scud.

'Not in battle, I take the tiller and Finn leads his fiercest warriors with sword and targe.'

'What about me?'

'When once you are accustomed to a craft like this you will take the tiller or be in command and take my place on this prow. You must use your brain in battle and your skill for sailing.'

They were soon there and made immediate arrangements to use the Dolmetron.

'What about Finn and the men? What will they do?' said Scud.

'Finn comes from a very old family and has an arrangement of his own. He will take the men with him and put the boat into a twilight world. I know how it works with the boat, but I cannot tell you yet of this. One day, perhaps.'

The wind was blowing off the sea and up in the Valley of the Stones it whistled through the polished hole. The cap was hovering and the force spreading to its outer limits.

'Now, Lord Scud, we will go under together. You have left a piece of hair in a safe place back in your village?'

'Yes, underneath the village stone.'

'Good. Under here then.'

Once beneath the slowly moving cap they felt the force penetrate every level of their being. It pressed in on them and tugged and pulled until suddenly, as if in a vacuum, all was still.

‘Well, that’s that then,’ said Scud. ‘When do we move off?’

‘You’re there. Look around.’

They were standing on a slope above a loch and just beyond them were the gates of a castle standing high and proud; the guardian of the entrance to the sea.

You are in Moidart at Castle Tioram.

‘I recognise it. It’s yours?’

‘And yours, Lord Scud, for as long as you want to stay here. Let us enter and take up our own.’

The Castle stood straight and upright in front of them perched on the rock above the loch. It seemed to grow from living rock straight up to battlements and other guarded places essential for defence. There was an entrance protected by a portcullis which they approached from what Scud took to be a pier.

‘The tide comes in high here, does it?’ said Scud.

‘We’re cut off most of the time,’ said the Christiana. ‘The whole area is an island. It’s deep enough for boats.’

The inside belied the strong, imposing, war-like image given to the world. There was a hall, a chapel, houses and what looked like the steading of a farm. It was a fortified village and Scud could see that folk lived here in comfort and not in some regimented place of arms.

Christiana led the way into a hall lit by flaming torches on the walls and covered in a glow from the kind of hearth a traveller likes to see.

‘We will go to our chambers first,’ said Christiana, ‘and then come back to meet your new friends and eat.’

Scud was home.

Chapter 46 The Old New World

He was received as one of them.

It was as if he had lived there all his life. When he entered at Christiana's side the assembled company rose and when he sat at her right hand, a noise – Scud thought it was a warning growl – came from a hundred throats to grow and grow until cheers and plaudits rent the air. He was Lord Scud, a sailor of renown, come home to aid their Queen.

A feast began and Scud had never seen such food. There was venison and salmon and roasted beef – roasted on the spit which stood in the central hearth. He could not recognise the half of it, but hunger overcame his doubts and patience.

Conversation filled the air and the noise increased until he thought his ears would burst. Acrobats and tumblers took the floor and then gave way to singers and a poet whose fiery exclamations sent Scud pulsing to the skies.

Not one to claim his bed if a company still held life, Scud felt he had to head upstairs if body and soul were still to be his own.

'You have had enough, Lord Scud?' said Finn attending to the needs of one whom he respected.

'If I'm to be ready for the morning, yes; I better get some sleep. A boat is ready for my use?'

'Aye and fifty of my best to help you try your skill. You do not mind if on this first sail, I come on aboard.'

'No, I welcome such as you to show me how she sails and if it comes to action with the brothers, it will be your sword and arm that will win the day because I could scarcely lift it. Such talent as I possess will never match the skills you offer to our Lady. But rest assured, you'll see me as a clear unfriend to those who cause her harm.'

A weary Scud fell into bed with thoughts coursing through his head. He never doubted that he had a part to play. He never doubted his acceptance and, in truth, that he belonged. The language too he found natural to speak and just before he fell asleep, he smiled at how the words and phrases of this land were fast becoming the natural way for him to speak.

In the morning the tide was in and a Dragon boat lay at the pier. She was a thing of beauty built for strength and speed. ADragon head was inlaid with gold and rose from a supple, almost flexing hull. There was a single mast stepped in the middle of the boat and a rectangle sail of red and blue. All was laid out for Lord Scud's inspection.

A pennon, embossed with the sign of the fish and longer than any flag Scud had ever seen, fluttered from the mast and proclaimed that this was the Lady Christiana's boat.

The sides were low, but right along both bulwarks hung shields, the rims, the studs and protruding boss of which were gilt in colour. Each represented not only a warrior and sailor, but a thegn, a man of rank, dedicated to the service of their Lady.

'There you are, my Lord,' said Finn of the Swords. 'She is the biggest in the fleet. – about 50 ells*.'

'How many sails does she have?' said Scud.

'Only one – a square sail. Oars are our strength. They give quick power when wind is scarce.'

'Tiring though,' said Scud. 'How long can they keep it up?'

'Not long at top speed but all day at a slower speed. The oarsmen are rested and we use the sail when we can.'

'How do you set the speed?'

'They all follow the oarsman nearest the bow – the stroke.'

'Where I come from we have a stroke but he sits at the stern. How do they follow someone they can't see?'

'Well raised, my Lord. He leads the rowing-chant and that sets the pace, but I well understand the point you make.'

'I think sails can be faster for long periods.' said Scud. 'Depends on your sail.'

'They are when there is a strong, following wind,' said Finn, ' but we do not sail well against the wind.'

**An ell is just under a metre.*

‘It’s because of the kind of sail you use. I’ve got three sails, one like yours and two that run up the middle of the boat.’

‘What good is that? You’ll never catch the wind.’

‘I can pull them out and in but there are specialist men for the sail, aren’t there?’

‘Yes, we angle the sail a bit and other men do that. Some bail out in bad weather and some operate the ropes holding up the sail and the mast. Everyman must fight. Nobody is just a sailor. Some are better sailors and some are better fighters.’

‘Will you take me out for a trial?’

Chapter 47 The Plan

Scud stepped aboard.

The men sat at benches at the oars. They appeared, at first, to be a wild looking bunch, but Scud knew that they were a stalwart, noble group of men, steadfast and strong and dedicated to their Lady.

'You are all well armed,' he said as he walked among them.

'We have to be, my Lord. You never know in these waters where the next attack will come from.'

'We have a good idea though,' said Finn coming up behind. 'As sure as God made night and day, it will be that Ruiri or Lachlan. Let the wings of the black beetle clear them from this place.'

'In these parts it is wise to be alert. Our enemies lie behind the headland and try to jump us as we pass. They have no chance. This is the fastest boat along these shores.'

'Ruiri and Lachlan are her two brothers?' said Scud.

'Aye and still out to get her throne.'

'They won't,' said Scud, 'but we've got to find a way to wreck them.'

'By the Sea-Runes, that we will,' said Finn.

The boat took off and flew before the wind, but when returning into the wind she lost her power. In that position she was a poor sailor.

'I see what you mean, Finn. She doesn't sail well to windward. This is a time for oars, is it?' said Scud.

'Yes, my Lord, if the brothers are after us.'

'Well, I don't know much about square sails like this, but I think it would go better if you loosened off the leading edge of the sail.'

Finn called to have it so and the boat improved.

'My Lord, it works. It looks all wrong but by my fathers it has a touch of magic in it. My Lady said you were a sailor. I have never seen the like.'

Scud took the tiller and gained a sense of what the boat could do. He learned how to use the oars and gloried in their pulsing beat. He liked to watch the arc they cast when rising all in line to pause before pulling down in one more sweep.

Then, on the outer circle of their sail and just before a headland only slightly higher than a lofty mast, two boats swooped into sight.

'By all that gives me strength,' called Finn, 'they think to try again.'

The Dragon boat swung round and with sails and oars they took off in clouds of spray and spume to gain the protection of their loch. Finn raised his horn and blew a long and booming blast to warn the castle of the danger.

'They will have the boom in place as soon as we clear its line and they may bang their bows against its strength.'

Arrows filled the air and trailed their smoking tails across the sky. Their plunging deaths far behind the racing Dragon were testimony to an effort failed.

Safe in Castle Tioram and looking down on the angry, bustling boats, Christiana laughed loud and clear. The brothers buzzed in vain and could find no satisfaction.

'Does this happen often?' said Scud.

'They keep trying.' said Finn, 'but in the end they leave and my Lady still reigns here. The brothers only hold sway on the other side of Ard na Murchan, but their Castle Mingary is very strong.'

'We should get it stopped, said Scud. 'How many boats have we got.'

'Two and a little ten-oared Birlinn. We have the biggest boat, but we are not strong enough to finish them off for good.'

'Have you tried to capture them?'

'Three times we have tried and three times they have fled with broken boats, but we durst not follow. The brothers come back and will not accept their rightful chief. Unless we can sack the Castle at Mingery we cannot force them to yield.'

'If we can destroy them at sea Mingary would not help them, would it?'

'In truth, you are right my Lord. Without sea-power they would submit. If we could destroy or capture their boats they would have to recognise their rightful Queen.'

'Well!'

'When we meet they always have twice our craft.'

'Uh-huh,' said Scud. 'We'll have to think about that.'

'They are not rogues, well maybe Lachlan. They just cannot accept that the Lady Christiana is the sovereign Queen and Chief.'

A plan was forming in Scud's mind.

Chapter 48 The Battle

Scud was ready.

'My Lady, mighty Finn of the Swords, I ask this of you. Are the brothers in command when the boats lie off your shores?'

'Yes,' Lord Scud, said Finn, 'but it is usually Ruiri. It is important to him that he is seen to defeat the Lady Christiana.'

'You have a plan, Lord Scud?' said Christiana.

'So his claim fails if you are seen to vanquish him.'

'Along with her possession of the Golden Helix, that is so.'

'Here then is what we do.'

Scud had spent the night working out how the battle should be fought.

'Before we ever take to water, to give ourselves an advantage, I want a second sail constructed and some alterations made to your Dragon boat.'

Scud had a jib cut out, a sail to be set right forward – the kind used in his time.

To Finn and all his sailors it seemed nonsense, a triangular scrap that looked tiny when compared with the huge, square, main sail used on all their boats.

'Where are we going to put that?' said Finn. 'It looks like a big flag.'

'It will pull right to the top of the mast and I want a pole fixed right out beyond the bow. We'll attach the bottom of the front edge of the new sail to it and bring the other end back to the gunwale to leave a gap between the two overlapping sails. When the wind rushes through it will speed up and the boat will go faster and closer to the wind.'

'It will get broken when the fighting starts,' said Finn.

'I know; but if it performs once in battle, as a surprise, we'll send one of their boats to hell,' said Scud.

'Ah,' said Finn, 'you see what he has in mind, my Lady?'

'Yes, I do and I know what it is called, "The Venturi Effect".'

Finn looked at her strangely, but said, 'with sails fixed like that, we . . .'

'By the Holy God of the Elements, 'if we can go much closer to them when they do not expect it, we will wreck them.'

'We will need arrows and fire and stones to heave when we are in close. No doubt you will be arranging all that. When all is ready, Finn, I will ask you to take a boat and hide it on the north side of our loch, there to stay until a beacon on our hill springs you forth. Our Dragon boat will similarly be stationed on the south side.'

'And now the bait: The Birlinn will sail south under a skilful captain flying our Lady's Pennant to suck forward their fastest boat – that of Ruiri.'

'Then we'll see: with Finn on the North side I'll come out behind him when he passes to trap him in a vice which will close fast.'

'And the rest of his fleet?' said Finn.

'Send men to the hill over-looking Mingary to light fires and shout and apparently threaten the castle and the harbour while the fleet is absent.

Some of his boats will turn back to fight off this threat but I judge that the impetuous Ruiri will not be able to resist the sight of the Lady Christiana in a ten-oared Birlinn. The safety of the Castle will be left to brother Lachlan and you, mighty Finn of the Swords, will take care of them when Ruiri is safely in our hands.'

'My Lord Scud,' said Christiana, 'Your plan will work, I know it, but where stand I. I am not accustomed to staying on the shore as you well know.'

'I hope you will command your boat, my Lady, and if you deem me worthy let me guide you as once before you guided me in a battle in my time. I have to ask that Finn should put another in his place to give you the safety of a strong right arm.'

That night and the days and nights which followed were used to ready for the battle.

Men set out for Mingary and a signal beacon was placed upon the hill above the Castle Tioram. The little Birlinn sailed as if without a care and out to take the air on a summer afternoon and flew its pennant streaming in the wind. Finn left quickly, his boat of 30 oars was smaller than the Dragon, but packed with men each one a warrior of repute. It sailed a course just off the shore ready to slam shut the northern door. Scud and Christiana took the Dragon boat south and in a handy inlet hid from the seaward side with branches from the coastal forest.

'We're ready, my Lady. Pray God he'll take the bait.'

'He will. Ruiri is consumed with envy and Lachlan is greedy.'

'We definitely face this Lachlan too.'

'We might but he'll likely be sent back to defend their stronghold. His interest is gold and silver and if Ruiri yields he'll disappear to other seas.'

Ever restless, Ruiri moved as soon as the Birlinn was spotted from his shores. His fleet of four sailed north but when Mingary was threatened two boats returned to ensure his base was secure. When the die was cast the Birlinn turned for home and drew Ruiri like a lure.

With the prize of Christiana shining in his eye, Ruiri played his part just as the script demanded. With shouts of triumph he plunged toward the tiny boat until, when opposite the mouth of Moidart Loch, he was aghast to see that it was not her at the helm. At that time the trap slammed shut.

Coming up behind, having ejected fast from their inlet cover, were Scud and Christiana and, to his front, Finn, alerted by a flaming beacon, was bearing down with all the power at his command. Scud, for Christiana had now passed all control to him, soon reached Ruiri's escort boat on a parallel course and into wind. With oars raised and with the new triangular sail the Dragon boat went tight and slammed into the smaller boat. The unexpected move reduced the craft into a bloody, screaming mangled mess as splintered, spearing oars reduced the crew into a porridge of the dead and dying. The boat swung round in hopeless disarray and when rained with stones and arrows, struck to yield in obeisance to their rightful Queen.

With the odds against him Ruiri tried to flee, but Finn's smaller, slower boat was in his path intent on boarding from the seaward side. Craving open water wherein to use his speed he turned to port but Finn struck his bow a glancing blow to turn him south again towards the charging Scud. In desperation, but now before the wind, he sought to re-organise his panic-stricken crew and reach the safety of the open sea.

Alas for him Scud saw the danger of sailing into wind against a boat with a broad sail filling both full and free. As Ruiri steered to cross his bow and flee Scud sailed tight to cross him by the stern. Judging speed and distance with accuracy of eye and hand he thrust an oar between his stern post and rudder to take away the power to steer. He was trapped now at bow and stern and with his life and all his dreams of kingly power forfeit, he yielded in submission to the will of the Lady Christiana.

The kingdom now is yours, my Queen and all within its bounds pay fealty to your grace.'

* * *

'Scud!' shouted Fergus. 'Where are you? It's the Queen's Cup. The sailing season starts today. Remember? Get up. You've got the biggest challenge of your life to win.'

'No, Fergus. I've won that already.'

BIOGRAPHIES – THE CALL OF THE HELIX

SCUD is the youngest of a sailing family. He is a born sailor and has ambitions to be a great one. He tells stories about a metaphysical, sailing queen called Christiana who is from the 14th century. Although he achieves maturity in her defence while in her time, he still struggles through adolescence in his own time.

FERGUS is the oldest of the sailing family and by far the most experienced sailor. Sailing brings out the positive side of his personality and allows him to support Scud's talent. Distrustful of supernatural assistance, he shows signs of faltering in the face of his young brother's challenge.

MAIRI is the cleverest of the siblings. Although Fergus is the sailing leader, she is the one who organises them and solves many of their problems. She sacrifices her own considerable sailing talent to help develop Scud's latent skills.

PETE is a complex mixture. He is fourth in the family by age, good with books and clever with his hands. Sailing is just one of his many interests. He looks like a medieval monk or a studious explorer and specialises in understanding nature and the past.

CHRISTIANA is a 700 years old who appears and disappears at will. Contact with her is difficult and only Scud knows what she looks like. He describes her as glowing, dressed as a warrior queen and a brilliant sailor. She is strong, determined and very helpful to Scud.

ANN is a friend and fellow sailor from the home village. She is tenacious, stubborn and very fit. She has a small, purple star at the corner of her mouth which glows when she gets angry and she can get very angry.

IAIN looks a bit like his sister, Mairi, but there the resemblance ends. He is very quiet, but when he speaks you realise that he knows what he is talking about.
RUIRI is Christiana's brother who seeks to usurp her throne.